LABOUNTY

LABOUNTY

A. ALEX COME'

ARPress
45 Dan Road Suite 5
Canton MA 02021
Hotline: 1(888) 821-0229
Fax: 1(508) 545-7580

Ordering Information:
Quantity sales. Special discounts are available on quantity purchases by corporations, associations, and others. For details, contact the publisher at the address above.

Printed in the United States of America.

ISBN-13:   Softcover   979-8-89330-093-2
             eBook   979-8-89330-095-6
             Hardback   979-8-89330-094-9

Library of Congress Control Number: 2024902519

Table of Contents

CHAPTER ONE

Jonathan Labounty was a lone rider and around him brewed a fierce Mountain Storm. The rain had not yet hit but filled the night air with the scent of closeness. Having ridden through many such squalls he held little worry.

Once the downpour began, it would hammer hard and carry with it a harsh bitter chill. The well-seasoned Buckskin Coat he wore was holding in the warmth, and the old slicker tied to the cantle would fend off the showering rain once it arrived. To him a Mountain Storm was invigorating. It kept his senses awakened.

Out of the darkness a small Fox scampered onto the shadowy path. Deciding to pause, it stood staring at the peculiar rider straddling the big animals' back. Reining-in his horse Labounty smiled speaking softly into the forest wind dancing through the trees, "I know what you're thinking Red", he told the little creature, "But I got to tell you. This human feels as at home here as you do". The thick tailed little critter raised his pointy ears and cocked his head, as if trying to decipher the words. But quickly realizing it impossible, he turned dashing back into the darkness from which he had come; no doubt heading for his den where he'd stay warm and dry till the angry world in which he lived calmed back down.

Resting his hands on the saddle horn, Labounty gave thought to the free-spirited little varmint. Here at home in the Sierra Nevada his life was harsh and high risk, but at the same time, to him satisfying. Shifting the sentiment to himself he admitted, his life below was little different. Running through his mind he considered an old saying he had heard long ago; one straight from the Good Book itself. Raising his eyes to Heaven he gave a jesting smile; "if I get it wrong, please don't knock me free of the saddle with a round of Fire. Lowering his head, he spoke once again into the wind now whistling stronger through the trees... The thing that hath been, it is that which shall be; and that which is done is that which shall be done: and there is no new thing under the sun. He recalled an old Padre's explanation of the verse: 'no matter' he had said, 'what be the color your skin or the country you come from, it will always be the same, loving, and hating, killing and helping, being rich or poor, tall or short, be you man or woman, young or old. Everywhere in God's earth these behaviors will always be, because his holy word tells us, the Devil is the Prince of the Air here, meaning, he is the one ruling this world. Hence, it will always be this way, until the day our Lord returns. So long as the Devil is in power, there will be nothing new under the sun.

To Labounty the explanation stuck. However, over the years he had tailored the Padre's explanation down to two words...human behavior!

Twisting in the saddle he glanced up into the night sky behind him. The storm had been chasing him for hours, its dark brooding threat steadily growing and speeding. He had watched its determined approach while enjoying the chase; now it had finally arrived. Light taps of rain had begun falling and he knew the hard hitters would soon follow.

Untying the slicker, he slipped it over the buckskin coat. He was a man of expectation. That was his way, how he lived: expect the worse, expect the best, expect nothing...but always expect something. The mountain creatures, like the inquisitive little Fox, thought him irrational, having long tucked themselves safely away in dens, beneath rock cliffs, caves and fallen trees well protected from another of nature's wild rages. But to him, this aspect of the Maker's Construction was precisely what he intended, wanted...to become a tiny speck lost within the expanse of

Mountain Wilderness, the perfect abode of beauty, amazement and with it the flair of danger.

That thought hit with a wake-up call…a sudden Streak of Lightening tore through the trees less than a hundred feet from the nose of the Paint, branches split, shattered and burned, the impulsive brilliance blinded Labounty and within seconds of darkness returning, thunder exploded like the Cannons of War he had spent years trying to forget. The deafening boom vibrated the ground frightening his mount and the pack mule towed behind. Hunching, the paint whinnied loud sidestepping with anxiety. Clutching the reins steadily, he leaned forward patting her neck and soothing her with soft words.

When her calm returned, he straightened into the saddle and opened his eyes to the firmament. It remained a chilling blackness void of stars with thin hazy clouds drifting over the face of a pale dour Moon.

From the trees leaped an intense gust of wind slapping at his hat and slicker. It was harsh but lasted only a few seconds. Across the mountain skies lightning continued as its wild flashes and rumbles of thunder heralded in the storm's unmistakable arrival. Both the Paint and long-eared pack-mule continued their dislike for any of it; especially the ear-piercing thunder shaking the world upon which they walked.

Labounty understood storms here in the high country were often intensified. Although the horse and mule were relentlessly spooked, and he was a lone isolated rider he remained calm, always respectful of the tempest's unforgiving dominance. He considered storms as just another display of the Great Maker's astonishing love for variety…and too, sometimes it took intense reminders as to who it is that remains in charge. Giving the Paint a soft touch from his heels they ambled forward.

The handsome square-jawed Engineer of rawboned muscle, soft auburn hair and eyes of gentle green gave a sigh. Despite the storm's chill, the soon arrival of a hard hammering rain, and a day or so before the warm Mountain Sun fell on his face while setting traps, he remained content; as he had told little Red. He too was home.

CHAPTER TWO

Because the hard rain was not far off, the necessity to camp had become a priority. For over an hour, he had been searching for the perfect spot, preferring a cabin or cave, but so far, he had come upon neither.

There was a story of a Black man venturing into the Sequoia Forest following the war. That he had built a cabin somewhere within its vast confines. His cabin would have been a welcome sight, but because of the forest's great expanse, the odds of stumbling upon it were as likely as finding a lost horseshoe in the middle of the Mojave.

A sudden increase in the cold taps of rain began to fall and at the same instant lightning flashed, silhouetting an ideal campsite amid a tight cluster of young Sequoia. Quickly, he reined in the animals there.

Dismounting, he untied a small wooden box from the pack-mule and pulled an oil lamp from it. When lit, he used the light to strip gear from both animals, stretched a rope between two trees and tethered them close and tight since he was in Paiute Country. He was not aware of any young, disheartened warriors AWOL from the reservation, but if so, and they were to stumble upon his camp, the Paint and Mule would hopefully give him a heads up.

Working quickly, he put together the framework of a lean-to using precut poles carried on the packsaddle, then stretched a canvas over it and tied it securely in place. While the wind hampered his efforts, he did appreciate the hard rain holding off.

Inside he built a soft bed of dry fern and spread a blanket over it. At the open face of the lean-to, he dug out a hole for the fire, and then banked it with short pieces of log for the confinement of added warmth. After collecting enough firewood for the night, he stacked it inside where it would remain dry.

By the time the rain hit he was inside the shelter boiling coffee and frying strips of bacon. The shielding of the trees kept out most of the wind and the warmth of the fire lingered pleasantly within the confines of the lean-to.

His gun belt hung within quick reach and the packsaddle with gear lay at the foot of his bed. Bacon crackled as it fried, and its aroma, along with that of the coffee teased his appetite. Sighing with contentment Johnathan Labounty grinned, what else could a man wish for. To him, this was Heaven on Earth.

Outside the shelter, darkness lay gentle with the wind continuing moaning through the trees. Rain splattered against the canvas and soft fire shadows flickered on the tapered wall behind him.

Propped against his saddle he poured a cup of coffee and sipped it slowly. Then broke out a piece of hardtack and ate it along with two strips of bacon. Nothing in the world he thought, short of sharing the coffee and bacon with the Maker himself, could match the tranquility of a Mountain retreat.

Of course, as was the case every year, the Railroad had pitched a fit saying they could not spare him the time off. Always, things were too busy, or they were too short-handed. And always each year he offered them his resignation as Chief Engineer and Surveyor. However, in every case the boss while chewing on his stubbed cigar grumbled, telling him to get the hell out but be back in four weeks.

Because he was a graduate of Harvard, had served as an engineer throughout the war and worked as a scout during the early Indian campaigns, they considered him irreplaceable. Such thinking, he felt, was worth smiling about; truth be known the railroad was filled with men who could do his job, at least most of it. A good worker yes, he was that, but irreplaceable… very few men were such.

When full, Labounty set the frying pan with three remaining strips of bacon to the side and refilled his coffee cup. The fern bed was of comfort, and he stretched out on his back with head resting on the Saddle.

Rain continued falling hard, crashing robustly through the trees and hammering the tarp; it was a relaxing sound. The thunder itself had quieted, diminishing to little more than distant rumblings. Even the lightning had eased its frequency. The worst of the storm seemed to be passing. Tonight, he thought he would sleep like a newborn.

A tiny droplet of rain fell into the fire, and it protested with an angry sputter. Then a twig snapped somewhere in the darkness behind the lean-to. Instantly he jerked the .44 Smith & Wesson from its holster. With his left leg he kicked out the fire; it died in seconds and a cold blackness swallowed the lean-to. Controlling his breathing, he listened. The only sound left was rain splattering the tarp.

Why had the Paint not warned him. The sound could have been a bear seeking shelter, or a Paiute warrior – or worse, a small party of them; but more likely, he reasoned, Indians had not made the sound, they would not have been that careless. The possibility of some smaller animal was out as well; to snap a twig big enough to hear over a falling rain took considerable weight and had to be close. It had to be a man!

He felt cold and shivered as the now bitter night air chased away the last of the lingering heat. Motionless, lying on his back, Labounty stared into the darkness above, then came the faint sound of another twig snapping. Whoever it was, they were closing in. Silence came again.

Gut instinct, as it had many times during the war sent an unexplained warning… get out! Gripping the butt of the .44 tightly, he quickly rolled free of the lean-to arching over the firewall. At the same instant two separate stabs of flame followed by the loud report of a rifle broke the night silence: the sound echoing loudly through the trees.

The slugs tore through the canvas and into the fern bed where he had been lying. Quickly he fired two shots of his own, aiming into the area where he'd caught a glimpse of muzzle flame through the white tarp. The cry of a man pierced the night and long before the pained voice fell silent, Labounty rolled twice more.

Lying motionless he caught another faint snap of a twig from the darkness to the front; so, he knew there were at least two people out there. Lightning lit up the woods, but he saw nothing. When darkness returned, he wiped water from his eyes.

His clothes were soaking wet, and he shivered. His eyes narrowed straining to see into the wet blackness. He wanted noise; something to hint of their position, but the forest gave up no sound, only wind and pattering rain.

Then to his right the Paint whinnied someone was there. Remaining still, he lay on his back, ears alert. Another shot erupted tearing into the tree only inches above his head. Tiny fragments of wet bark splattered his face but caused no injury.

Through the years, he had come to learn life was but a random run of luck, risks and gambles. In split second reasoning, he chose to gamble now. In a voice just loud enough to be heard above the wind, he cried out as though he had been hit and remained motionless, waiting.

Rain continued falling, bombarding the already soaked ferns in which he lay. His hair was soddening against his head and water ran steadily down his face. Anxiety was high but he kept it in check. Patience thinned quickly; but within seconds, his hunch paid off. A voice somewhere in the darkness to his front called out, and it was a welcomed relief.

"I think I got him, Red. I think the son-o-bitch is dead."

To the speaker's left another man replied.

"Well go see ya old goat. He's already kilt Sticky so be careful." Eyes now more adjusted to the darkness, Labounty watched as an indistinguishable form zigzagged toward his position. With the worst part of the storm waning, the moon had begun to show life. Gaps in the tops of the trees allowed a pale gray light to filter in amid the rain.

The second man Labounty waited to shoot advanced through a series of the blotched Moon light. But because the trees were grouped close, he was visible one second, out of sight the next. Forcing his patience he waited, eyes straining while glued to the pathway down which the man approached. Constantly water ran into Labounty's eyes, and he wished he had his hat. But he dared not move; for the slightest stir might hint he was alive and waiting.

With careful calculation, he picked a small clear spot straight-ahead, one through which the approaching man would eventually run. This would be the best shot he could have, and the stranger would be dangerously close when he fired.

Arm stretched with the butt of the revolver resting on the ground he pulled back the hammer and held steady. He hoped lightning did not flash before he got off the shot. If the killer were to see him stretched out and waiting, it would nix everything.

Forcing calm he waited, the barrel of the revolver pointed and ready. Then the man was there. Labounty fired twice and immediately rolled to the right, listening as the shots he fired raced away through the soggy woods. Lightning flashed, a second-long burst and he caught a glimpse of the stranger falling face first into the wet ferns. Darkness swallowed them again.

Listening intently, Labounty laid stomach down and motionless. There were no sounds out of the ordinary, but he knew at least one more person remained.

This was all so senseless. He hated killing. He had had more than his share during the war, taking the lives of fellow Americans, with far too many little more than boys barely in their teens.

The Indian wars had been no different, with the too-often needless slaughter of innocent Indian women and children. Twice he had come close to court-martial for refusing participation in what he considered nothing more than cold-blooded murderous raids. Now, because of it all, he lived with far too many bitter memories.

"Hey you."

The voice originated from near the Horse and Mule, but the man moved as he talked. "I ain't got no fight with you. You just kilt the old man but that was no great loss. Hell, he was worthless as hot horseshit served to a starvin' man."

As the outsider talked and moved, Labounty easily figured out his strategy; he was working his way around behind.

"Mister," he continued, "alls I care about is havin' me a cup of your hot coffee. What do ya say we make us a truce?"

The circling killer fell silent then and suddenly Labounty realized the rain had returned to a light drizzle. The wind had quieted too but continued moaning softly.

The deadly game was building toward a climax, it appeared only Labounty, and one player remained, although he could not be certain. Rising quickly Labounty dashed deeper into the trees away from the campsite. The wet ground was both a blessing and curse. While it helped him move in near total silence, it did the same for the man who was trying to put a bullet in his back.

Gunfire erupted again and he dove for the ground, but this time he was not so lucky. The hot chunk of lead sliced through the muscle on the back of his neck. It was deep and he cursed the stinging pain as warm blood rolled down his back. The man was a good shot. Then two more rounds followed, flying out of the darkness zinging past his cheek. Immediately he fanned off two shots of his own and crawled to the far side of the horse and mule. There he took a moment to listen.

Satisfied, he lifted himself swiftly, ran a short distance and dove behind a tangle of tree roots. Like his hat, his pistol belt was in the lean-to, and he had fired six shots; his gun was empty. Somehow, Labounty knew his stalker was thinking the same thing, and he envisioned the killer smiling because of it.

But inside, Labounty was smiling too. Reaching into the upper inside of his boot, he retrieved six shells from the special webbing. Quickly he pushed the gun's top-break release, allowing the cylinder and barrel to pivot downward automatically ejecting the six spent cartridges. With cold fingers, he replaced the rounds and snapped the weapon back together. Every pair of boots he owned had been modified to hold six rounds for the Smith & Wesson. The gun itself had been recommend by two good friends, Wyatt Errp and Wild Bill Hickcock. It had also proven itself a faithful companion through the Indiana Wars. The spare rounds sown into the lining of his boots had come in handy as well. It was something he had done since he was old enough to buy his own. The practice had saved his life twice before, and tonight, he hoped would prove number three.

With the back of his hand, he swiped water from his eyes, and before he finished the stranger was there, standing just behind him with rifle leveled. Moving slowly, Labounty pulled himself around into a sitting position facing him while placing his back against the muddied roots of the fallen tree, then he looked up.

A dark, vaguely distinguishable form stood towering over him. There was a long awkward silence. Then a flash of lightning lit the darkness and for a second, Labounty glimpsed his would-be killer.

He was a mountain man in furs and buckskin. And he was grinning through a long, unkempt beard with a mouth of missing teeth. Then the light was gone. The mountain man spoke into the returning darkness, flippant, and as he talked, Labounty slowly pointed his pistol to the man's chest.

"Hell, and dark damnation stranger", the man began, "I reckon things don't look too good fer you, now do they?"

"No." Labounty told him. "So why don't you and I go get that cup of my hot coffee, because to tell the truth, things don't look good for either one of us."

The stranger laughed into the faded light. "I like your salt mister. But you seem to be the only feller' that things don't look good for. And I got to tell ya, all this talkin' ain't gonna' help ya none. Cause I'm gonna' gut shoot ya, then take everything ya own fer my own, whilst you lay out here on this wet ground dyin' and thinkin' bout it."

Labounty fired twice, both slugs tearing hard into the mountain man's chest. Through the dim darkness, he watched the hazy form pedal backwards as if trying to maintain his balance, and then fall onto his back into the cold ferns.

Gun ready Labounty moved quickly to his side. The rifle was still in his left hand so kneeling, he grabbed it and threw it out of reach. Lightning flashed again and he saw the stranger staring up at him. The bearded man groaned, and with his last ounce of strength, he grasped Labounty's arm. Despite his voice gurgling from the blood filling his throat, Labounty was able to make out his last words.

"Six shots, that's what ya fired. I counted em. You ain't got no gun bel... he gurgled one last time and he was dead.

The woods remained quiet except for the cry of the soft wind. The rain had stopped. That was good, but things were not as they should be. Frowning Labounty turned to study the Lean-to. The fire was burning again. Someone had rekindled it.

CHAPTER THREE

Utilizing trees for cover Labounty worked his way to the front of the lean-to. Ten yards out, he knelt concealed by brush and furn. Someone sat huddled in front of the fire partially hidden behind the log bank; he could not make out their face or if they held a gun.

Whoever it was sat staring into the yellow flames; something a smart man would never do, especially if he planned to kill someone coming in from the dark. Labounty could smell the bacon and knew they had set the pan and coffee back over the fire for re-warming.

Was it a trap, a trick to draw him out of the shadows, with someone else waiting to shoot him in the back? Except for a softened wind, quiet enough to hear the crackling of the fire, all seemed natural. Above the trees, a now near full moon shown bright and a whisper of stars were beginning to twinkle down at the world.

Minutes crawled by as he lay silent in the darkness, watching. Uneasiness lingered. There was no way of knowing for sure how many of these men there were? So far, he had killed three, and now a fourth sat huddled around his fire.

To Labounty it seemed pointless just lying there; a stalemate could end up lasting hours, the situation required a little prodding. With the .44 ready, he called out from where he lay, "You there, by the fire!"

Whoever it was jumped, his words had startled them. Turning, they squinted out into the darkness. Labounty frowned whispering under his breath, "what the…!" The man at the fire was no man at all; he was a small boy.

Remaining motionless, Labounty took in what he could see. The youngster wore a black Padra Hat with a tall feather stuck in the band. The hat was far too large for his head and sat resting on his ears, pushing them out like a pair of over-sized kites. Labounty grinned but it left quickly.

Beneath the mammoth hat uneasiness showed on the youngster's face, but it changed quickly to a calculated smile. The boy spoke loudly. "Hot damn Mister", he said squinting for a visual of where Labounty lay, "did you have to scare me like that? I damn near filled my britches." The boy paused, waiting for a reply, but Labounty remained silent.

The youngster spoke again. "Mister, sure as horses shit balls, it's safe to come on in and have you a slice of hog. Ain't nothin' like the taste of porker meat warmed over."

Choosing to remain silent, at least for a while longer, Labounty took in the sounds around him. He heard nothing out of the ordinary and the only activity seemed to be that at the lean-to. The boy spoke out once more, his voice edged with nervousness, his grin gone.

"My name's Cub. Them three you shot was no counts anyhow. Treated me like dog puke served on a fancy dinner plate," the boy paused then added, "course, reckon I didn't treat them no better, I didn't like em." He laughed a little, just for an instant, then his face went sober again, "Really Mister, you done this here territory a big, fat favor. They were all dumb as a box of rocks, and useful as a pair of old boots that ain't got no bottoms."

The boy named Cub blinked his eyes. His pupils were adjusting to the darkness now and he stared into the area where Labounty lay. Growing fidgety, he spoke a fourth time, irritation obvious.

"Mister, you not sayin' nothin' is gettin' on my nerves. Say somethin' to me. Call me stupid brain, puke face, buffalo dong, hell, it doesn't make no never mind, I don't care, just say somethin', will ya?"

Labounty did not find the boy's vocabulary at all suitable, and it seemed to be getting worse. So satisfied it was not a set up, he rose from where he lay and walked cautiously to the lean-to. The boy's eyes stayed with him every step of the way.

When he reached the entrance, he stopped, staring down at the kid with the Outhouse mouth. The boy glanced first at the .44 gripped in Labounty's hand, then slowly raised his eyes to Labounty's. Following a moment of silent staring, Cub bit thoughtfully at his bottom lip and asked, "You gonna' shoot me?"

Staring deadpan into the boy's wondering eyes, Labounty told him, "Not unless you've drunk all the coffee."

"Hot Damn, am I glad." Cub practically shouted the words.

Labounty crawled into the lean-to and replaced the two empty rounds in the Colt then stuck it back in the hanging holster. Silent, the boy watched his every move. Rummaging through the packsaddle he removed a towel and small tin of salve. Pouring water on a corner of the Towel, he cleaned the wound on his neck then applied a layer of salve. When finished he placed the tin back in the pack and hung the towel up too dry. He then made himself comfortable on the bed of ferns and looked the boy over.

The youngster's face lay covered with days of dirt, probably weeks, maybe months, maybe a year or more. His clothes were no different. Wearing a well warn duster twice his size he smelled to high heaven. A pair of bright blue eyes, however, sparkled in the firelight; and they were young eyes alive with adventure and curiosity. Sadly, he saw no sign of a boy raised in a good home; this young fellow had been kicked around living with the pain of growing up hard. His language, clothes and body all needed a good cleaning. However, once that was all done, Labounty guessed he'd find a cute little rascal with dimples and shaggy blond hair… or at least he guessed it to be blond; it was difficult to tell.

All the while Labounty looked him over, the youngster's face was growing tense. So, feeling he had unsettled him enough, Labounty began a conversation, "So, Cub is your name, hey son?"

"Yes sir," the boy said with a guarded nod.

"Well, they call me Jonathan Labounty." Following that with a grin of goodwill, he reached out his hand to the boy for a shake. The youngster was stunned, staring at the big hand stretched before him. Long seconds of pondering raced through the boy's mind; then his blue eyes lifted slowly to stare at Labounty. As if an explosion of unprecedented relief had detonated, his little hand shot out and grasped Labounty's.

"Hot damn," he said with a flush of relief radiating beneath the dirty face "I surely am glad you're actin' friendly. And gladder more, mind ya, that ya ain't gonna' shoot me." Releasing his grip Cub turned enthusiastically to the fire and grabbed the Frying Pan. "Here," he said turning to Labounty, "There's three hog slices left, go on and take em, but be careful, they be mighty hot."

Labounty declined thoughtfully, figuring the boy needed them much more than he did.

As the youngster ate, he watched with a grin, the boy's eating manners certainly gave his vocabulary competition; somewhere along the line he had forgotten how to chew. Handing Cub, a piece of hardtack to go with the bacon, Labounty poured himself a cup of coffee.

Settling back, he took a sip listening to sounds outside the lean-to. The rain had begun again, a soft easy fall pecking away at the tarp. Far off, somewhere over a distant slope, a silent streak of lightning flashed. The wind had picked up some and howled through the creaking trees. The boy belched. Looking at Labounty he wiped his mouth with his coat sleeve and smiled, "Mister," he said, "that was some eatin' and I thank ya. You got yourself a heart bigger than a fat saloon girl's ass."

That was it! Labounty had had enough of the nasty mouth. Reaching out he grabbed the youngster's arm and pulled him close, "And you, young man, have a mouth as dirty as a coal miner's... face."

The boy developed a shocked expression, but Labounty continued. "I realize I do not know you, but I'm saying it, you use that kind of language again and I'll see to it you cannot sit a saddle for a week. You understand?"

Astonishment showed on the boy's face as he stared silently into the eyes of the man gripping his arm, wondering just how far he dare go. Then words shot out of his mouth like a Bee ready to sting; "Hellfire and Brimstone Jonathan Labounty, what's the big fat deal? Old Red and them talked like that, and they never got huffy. They thought it was kinda' funny when I copied em."

"Well, I do not find it a bit funny. Foul language from the mouth of a small boy contains no humor whatsoever."

Cub grew red faced and pointed a finger "Hold on Mister, I ain't no small boy. I'm ten, almost eleven and I can take care of myself."

"FINE!" Labounty said letting go of his arm. "Then take this and make a bed for yourself." He threw the boy a blanket and continued, "I'm going out to bury your friends. While I'm gone, tend to the fire and be thinking about cleaning up your language."

Grabbing his gun-belt, a lantern and shovel, Labounty climbed out of the lean-to. The rain was still falling at a drizzle. Pausing, he looked down at the boy then up into the night sky, breathing in the fresh Mountain Air. He did not like to do what he was about to do, but it was only right. He was never one to leave a human body to be feasted on.

It took a little over an hour to bury the three men. When he returned, Cub was lying on his back staring into the ceiling of the lean-to. Continuing to stare up, not looking at Labounty he spoke, "I would a helped if ya asked".

"Thanks", Labounty told him warmly, "but I figured with them being your friends and all, not being part of it would be easier on you."

"I reckon it was", Cub said in a near whisper, continuing to stare up at the ceiling, "Sorry about how I talk".

"Apology accepted." Labounty said.

The youngster pulled his blanket tight around him and curled onto his side. Nothing more was said, and he had drifted away in minutes.

For a long while, Labounty studied the slumbering youngster, wondering just what his story was? He was so young; did he even have parents or a home at one time? Was there even a place for him to go? These were all questions needing answers, however, not tonight he thought. Tomorrow would supply plenty of opportunity. Like the boy, he needed to sleep himself.

Pulling his blanket around his shoulders, he pillowed his head against his saddle and closed his eyes. The fire crackled softly, and a gentle steady bombardment of raindrops fell through the trees tapping the canvas. Such, he thought to himself, was the sound of Nature's Music, a composition produced by the Maker Himself.

Labounty's mind began drifting away with one final thought dancing in his head: THE BOY! His language was deplorable, encrusted dirt disgusting, and the near intolerable reek of unwashed clothes rancid. All of it in need of change. But there was one thing suitable…his name! CUB! Somehow it fit him.

CHAPTER FOUR

Upon awakening, Labounty found the skyline etched in crimson. In the middle of a yawn, he sat up quickly. The boy was gone! The first reaction was worry, then anger. Checking his firearms and finding them intact relief surfaced. Brisk morning air nipped at his face.

Throwing off his blanket, he rose to his knees and peered around the corner of the lean-to. Both animals remained tethered in morning shadows. Relieved again, he took time to stretch and yawn again.

'So, the boy had run off! He thought. Well, he would not get far traveling on foot in Mountain Terrain. The idea of him being alone did raise concern; this wilderness was no place for a small kid to be by himself. After breakfast, he'd break camp and track him; that should not prove a problem. The real concern was what to do once he had him back?

Although small, fire flames still flickered, he threw on one of the three remaining logs he warmed his hands while thinking; fate certainly had an inimitable way of ruining a man's treasured refuge. That kid! He knew little about caring for a young boy; but like it or not, he was now morally obliged to do something with him.

Looking up into the morning Sky, he bantered with the Maker, 'so, mind telling me what I did to deserve this manner of malevolent punishment? I was one man alone in this huge Forest covered Mountain, atop the world minding my own business. A lone single rider, miles upon miles from anyone and any place; THEN suddenly, It's Surprise Jonathan! And you dump right into my lap, a kid that smells to high Heaven with a dirt-filled vocabulary the size of Hell!

Shaking his head, Labounty pulled his eyes to the eastern sky. A giant yellow Orb, bright and perfectly round, was rising at the far end of the world spilling its warmth and precious daylight over endless miles of timbered slopes. Such bravura, Labounty marveled, was proof indisputably that a Creator did exist; despite that Creator dumping a 'dirty mouthed, dirty clothed and dirty skinned kid on him, right here on top of the world, where he was seeking only peace, tranquility and a four week stay at the grand Hotel known to him as Heaven on Earth. But no, now it had become Heaven and little Satan Hotel on earth! Closing his eyes, he sighed!

Birds fluttered cheerfully amid the Sequoia, singing chirps of appreciation for the sun's splendor and welcomed warmth. A troubled night was giving birth to a potentially decent new day; and yes, despite the night's clamorous interlude and bullet-graze on the back of his neck, he was thankful to be part of it.

Throwing the last two logs on the fire, he removed a can of beans and hand full of bacon bits from the packsaddle. After mixing them together in the skillet, he set it over the fire. He then added fresh ground to the coffee pot and set it over the fire. After adding four slices of thick bacon to the mix in the pan, he sat back and relaxed.

The fire snapped as it burned, and the pleasant smell of bacon and wood-smoke eased his anxiety. He wondered of the boy. What was to be done with him? Perhaps he should have begun tracking immediately upon waking - what if something happened before he found him? Seconds of thought passed before shaking his head lighthearted, 'No not to this kid. He was far too ornery to not remain safe; and besides, the youngster needed to learn life was not a game; that picking and choosing only that which you felt like doing was not always an option. Allowing him to taste the fright of being lost could prove a valuable lesson; might even cultivate the thought of respect and a sense of responsibility.

The coffee began to simmer. Anticipating the joy of the first sip Labounty leaned forward and sniffed the rising aroma. To a Lady, the rich fragrance of a bouquet of Red Roses would equal his liking to the scent of Mountain brewed coffee over an open fire.

"Hot damn Jonathan Labounty, you got that coffee and Beacon smellin' right good."

The little voice took him by surprise. Peering over the log bank Labounty let out a soft sigh of relief, with an unexpected flutter of joy too.

Cub was walking in pulling four-saddled horses. With or without them at tow, Labounty would have been pleased, not just because he had been spared the task of tracking the youngster, but because the rascal had returned safe and unharmed.

Pouring a cup of the hot coffee Labounty watched the kid tie up the horses. So, he hadn't run away after all. Last night he had thought the boy to be bigger, but the sight of the four horses towering over him now showed how small and fragile the kid really was.

His Duster dragged the ground, and it was surprising he wasn't tripping over it. The sleeves were rolled up several times to make way for his little hands, and the big hat was still pushing out his ears. The dirt on his face appeared worse than Labounty had first noticed. And the kid was in desperate need of a haircut - not to mention the need of a long bath with a Bucket of Soap. How in the world, he wondered, could a little kid come to smell worse than the Cheyenne Cattle Yards?

Labounty settled against his saddle as the boy entered, knelt and warmed his hands. Looking straight into Labounty's eyes he said with earnest, "Ya know, just as sure as the Devil's got a red pecker, you're lookin' at one hungry man. Cannot wait to taste that, Bacon. You were sleepin' right peaceful this mornin', so I went and got the horses. Figured it'd be a right big sin to wake ya. So, I just snuck out".

The boy glanced into the frying pan, licked his lips then looked back to Labounty, "You thought I run off, didn't ya?"

"Cub, let me tell you something" Labounty began," these mountains are filled with bears, mountain lion and wolves. Each a killer of men, and all when hungry would rip you apart and drag you home to their hungry babies. If you think you're big enough to handle them, then you have the right to be calling yourself a man. But short of giving you a lecture let me say this; surviving in this world isn't just a matter of being big or having lots of muscles, you need common sense and self-control to even it all out."

Labounty paused, wondering if the boy was grasping what he was saying. "Self-control is a necessary element to any man's success, not to mention his longevity." Cub frowned, his failure to understand the meaning of longevity was obvious.

Labounty clarified the word. "Longevity means to live a long life". The boy nodded, and Labounty continued. "Take for example your mouth, your bad language and sass. Not a good thing to be doing at your age, or any age for that matter, especially here in the west where everyone carries a gun."

Cub was chewing on his lip, mulling over what Labounty was saying and remaining quiet. "And common sense", Labounty continued, "or the lack of it, like going after those horses by yourself, unarmed and alone. That was just not smart".

Cub raised his hand, signaling Labounty to hush his talking. Beaming as though he had just won a debating contest, the boy opened his overcoat and displayed the big six-gun strapped over his shoulder. The huge iron hung clear to his knee.

Labounty's eyes moved from it to the boy's face, speaking harshly, motivated by a now grave worry for the youngster's safety.

"Boy," Labounty snapped, "what are you doing wearing that gun? Take it off right now."

Cub lost his grin and retorted hotly.

"You go to hell and kiss the right cheek of my ass on your way down!"

That was it! Anger boiled Labounty's blood. It was time for a lesson in manners, a spanking hard enough to redden both his cheeks. Scrambling to his knees for a grab of the boy's arm, Labounty struck the top of his head on a roof pole. The pain was instant. His hand shot to the top of his head, and he yelled, 'Damn it!"

Cub jumped on that right away pointing an accusing finger.

"See! You ain't no different. Me and you are like two ticks suckin' blood from a coon dog's ass; you're a swearin' man too."

"That's different." Labounty shouted.

"How?" Cub shouted back.

"Because I happen to be an adult."

"So, what. Big fat deal."

Labounty, now pointing his finger retorted, "The only big fat deal around here is going to be me blistering your butt. Now take that gun off like I said, or this adult will take it off for you."

Realizing Labounty meant business Cub's little hands worked furiously at the big buckle. There was anger on his face though; and when he handed it to Labounty he was not without words.

"And just what am I supposed to do if we meet up with Injuns? Let em' cut off my ears or worse yet, cut off my dinger and stuff it in my mouth like they done Custer's men? I heard the old man say he saw that done to a Miner once, in a place called Alaski. And they cut off his head and hung it top their lodge pole. Hellfire Jonathan Labounty, I got the right to be callin' myself a man, ifin' I want. And just like you done said, men wear guns, especially here in the west."

"Look," Labounty injected, trying to calm down, "if we do meet up with Indians you will have a better chance of staying alive without a weapon in your hand. Now stop acting like a little Schoolgirl and listen to what I am telling you. How old did you say you were anyway, six?"

The boy shouted back without hesitation. "Almost eleven, I done told you that already. And I've shot guns before."

"Oh, you have, have you?"

"Yeah!" Cub snapped, "Lots of times".

"Well answer me this mister big-little man. Have you ever been shot by one?"

The boy started to speak but caught his words. Turning he stood, kicked angrily at the ground with his boot toe and stormed off.

Feeling as though he had both won and lost that battle, Labounty pulled his knife and stirred the mix smoking in the pan.

Cub was standing with his back to him just a few feet from camp. His arms were folded expressing his anger, and he stood staring down at the ground. Labounty wondered if he was crying. Again, he wondered what he was going to do with this kid? How could he reach him? The fact that the boy needed a good whipping was a truism, but equally, he needed a show of kindness and understanding too, not to mention the virtue of patience. Continuing to stir the beans and bacon Labounty asked, "You have any kin folk, Cub?"

The boy spoke keeping his back to him. "Yeah, I got an aunt and uncle somewhere in Yuma. Farmers, I think? I never met em' but my Pa had talked about em' just before he…" Whirling around Cub looked sternly at Labounty. "What the hell you askin' about my kin fer'? You ain't thinkin' about takin' me there are ya?" There was noted anger in his voice, perhaps even a hint of pleading. "Mister", Cub went on, "I ain't cut out to be livin' like that, with some old man and woman frettin' over me all the time. Hell, I'd have to go to some dumb school with a bunch of corny girls and sissy boys. I'm telling ya, if that's what you're thinkin', just forget it. I'll be gone the first time you go out behind the bushes or go to sleep."

Labounty closed his eyes, biting his tongue over the language. Calmly as possible he continued to stir breakfast, careful not to show expression. He knew what to do now, what had to be done, there was no choice. He couldn't just leave the boy to fend for himself; he'd be dead within a week.

And he couldn't keep him with him; a ten-year old kid would just be in the way. Besides, his nerves would never hold up.

A few days ride to Yuma, he thought, deliver the boy then return right back here. It was a simple plan, a reasonably simple chore, and a positive answer to his dilemma. Wrapping a bandanna around the handle of the hot pan Labounty lifted it up and smiled, "Come grab a plate Cub, breakfast is ready". Together they ate in silence, each lost in their own thoughts. Labounty wondered how he was going to keep the kid corralled. He couldn't tie him to the saddle like a common criminal, as that would be cruel. Once they were out of the mountains and into the desert there would be no place for him to run. And even if he did, catching him would prove no chore.

Labounty looked at Cub's sad angry face and sighed. He was sympathetic for the youngster but taking him to Yuma was the only alternative. The kid would be far better off living a family life, gaining an education and developing friendships with good kids his age. Right now, he was too young to see it, but the day would come when he would.

Cub ate his beans and bacon more out of habit than taste. He was too angry to enjoy them; he knew Jonathan Labounty was planning to take him to Yuma. Why had he opened his big fat mouth about havin' kin? And school? The boy shuttered; Jonathan Labounty was like all the other grownups he'd been told about. Old Red had warned him often enough, telling how rich folk was always thinkin' they was better with all their book learnin' and highfalutin' ways. This Mr. Labounty was thinking of turning him into one of his kind. Well, he wasn't cut out fer it. Hell, he was a real man, and he planned to stay that way.

Slamming down his fork Cub broke the silence between them. When he spoke, his words crackled. Labounty was not sure if it was anger, or the boy was on the verge of tears. Either way, words became heartfelt.

"Please Jonathan Labounty, let me stay with you. I'll be good. I'll do everything I'm told. Just don't take me to Yuma." The youngster paused, looked down at his plate then back to Labounty, his eyes were wet.

"I'll tell ya Mister Labounty, in all honest truth, me livin' in Yuma would be like a stud stallion thrown into a pasture of hee-hawin' jackasses."

Speechless, Labounty stared at the boy. Then calmly he set down his plate. He refilled his coffee cup and leaned against his saddle. Thoughtfully he shook his head. Inside he was not sure if he wanted to laugh or cry. He did neither, he simply shook his head and asked The Maker above the big question; "Why me?"

CHAPTER
FIVE

Labounty and Cub broke camp around eight-thirty. Together, they disassembled the lean-to, securing the frame-poles inside the folded tarp, buried all refuse leaving nothing to scar the natural beauty of the area.

After retaining the best of the four extra mounts for Cub, Labounty turned the others loose. The ride to Yuma would require crossing miles of desert, water would be scarce, and there was no advantage in risking their lives watering horses they did not need.

"Besides", Labounty told the boy as he unsaddled them, "they'll be much happier here in the mountains running free".

By two that afternoon, they had descended the steep slopes and entered the valley floor. In the lead, Labounty pulled the pack-mule while Cub followed behind.

Here there was no place for the boy to run so Labounty rode easy. He hoped allowing Cub to ride tail would build trust in their relationship, explaining the position brought with it great responsibility; that of ensuring no one rode up behind them unsuspecting.

Out from the protective shade of the tall Sequoia the sun's searing rays beat down on their backs. The ride was hot but on the good side, the same breeze waving through fields of tall grass and flowers also cooled their skin. Clusters of Blue Spruce spotted the vast openness and quite frequently they startled feeding deer.

Labounty held an appreciation for the beauty surrounding them. He saw the Maker as an artist and counted the colorful mountain valley as one of His greatest works. He sat easy in the saddle. There were those who had no belief in the Maker, or an afterlife for that matter, claiming earth itself was man's Heaven or Hell. He saw such thinking as nonsense. Even if such a belief turned out true and this life was a cowboy's only ride; at least for one month out of every year he lived in Heaven; and would continue to do so until the day he breathed his last.

Turning, he glanced back at the boy. The youngster was still following, sitting in his saddle with one leg wrapped around the horn. He had hoped the boy would be no problem, and so far, he hadn't. Facing back Labounty pulled his hat from his head and wiped sweat from his brow.

To be completely free of the mountains would require at least one more night of camping – one more night in a place flourishing with fresh provisions; after that they would enter the desert, and everything would change. The terrain would become a flat, dry parched world virtually free of both food and water, not to mention lack of shade and cool breezes. If luck held and they ran into no trouble they would reach Yuma in a two- or three-day ride. The desert would present its own set of dangers and they would need to remain cautious. Aside from Indians the idea of their canteens going dry concerned him most.

Glancing into the blue sky he spoke softly to himself. "Before you worry over the dangers of the desert, Labounty, better stay focused on those at present."

While the mass of Indians had settled peacefully upon reservations, scattered throughout the area were small bands of hostiles, the resisters who would not, or could not give up the freedom that had been theirs for so long. In addition, what he had told Cub about bears and mountain lions was in fact true. And although rare, wild wolves would not hesitate to attack if hungry.

He was also troubled over the possibility of the boy getting hurt, perhaps breaking a leg or an arm or some such thing; if he did there would be no doctor to call on for help. Such possibilities were of no great concern when it was just, him alone, but with a small boy to care for it created an entirely different perspective.

Around four they came upon a wide stream and allowed the horses to drink. While sitting in their saddles the animals dunked their muzzles in the cool water. The spot was nicely shaded by Juniper and felt cool on the skin.

Upstream to their left a huge Elk Bull with a giant rack began to cross but stopped near midstream and sniffed the air. Picking up their scent it bolted away disappearing into a patch of thick brush.

Cub and Labounty listened for some time as it crashed its way along breaking twigs and branches noisily. Looking at Labounty Cub smiled, taken in by the splendor of the scene. Labounty smiled back with a nod. The stream gurgled softly over the rocks and a gentle breeze made the Juniper leaves chime.

Dismounting, Labounty untied a flap and began rummaging through the packsaddle. Cub watched him curiously. When he found what he was searching for he turned and threw it to Cub saying.

"Here, in case you've never seen one of those, it's a bar of soap. I want everything off and make sure you wash behind your ears. As soon as you have yourself scrubbed, then wash those God-awful smelling clothes you're wearing."

The boy opened his mouth to protest but Labounty stopped him.

"Do it, or I'll do it for you."

Angrily, his face twisted, Cub climbed down from the saddle and removed his clothes. Throwing a mean glance at Labounty, he splashed off naked to the middle of the stream where he flopped himself down in an expressively woeful manner. "Satisfied?" He shouted.

Labounty nodded, "Yes. Now scrub." Turning from the boy he sat and rested, smiling.

Overall, the bath and clothes washing took about twenty minutes. When Cub came out of the water Labounty wrapped a warm blanket around him.

"Feel better?"

"No!" the boy snapped, "it doesn't feel natural."

"Maybe not", Labounty said drying the youngster's back with some of the blanket, "but you sure as heck smell a great deal better."

As the boy re-dressed into his wet, but now clean clothes, he asked.

"Have you ever been here before Mister Labounty?"

The youngster's willingness to talk made Labounty feel good, and he took it as a promising sign. And the youngster beginning to call him Mr. Labounty was a bit encouraging.

"No Cub", Labounty answered", "not in this spot specifically. But I've been to this area several times. I've also been to the Rockies in Colorado, the Bitter Route Range in Wyoming territory, and the Great Smoky Mountains in Northern Virginia. And once, a long time ago when I was a young man not much older than you are now, I sailed with my father across the Pacific to the country of Japan where we back-packed up Mount Fuji."

Cub's eyes were big and filled with interest. "Wow", he said with fascination, "you been to Japan? What's it like there? Do they live like us? I mean with their squinty eyes and weird way of dressin' and all. They sure are strange folk".

The boy ran his fingers through his wet hair to push it back against his head and out of his eyes. "Me", he continued coolly, "I'm a travelin' man too. Been to Mexico twice. And once in Saint Louie, whilst Red and them was doin' it in a whorehouse, I talked a spell with a nigger fella from Afferca. He worked there at the whore house; he was the one that throwed out them that hurt the ladies".

Labounty shook his head in disbelief, wondering why anyone would take a small boy to such a place. Then he explained, "The man you talked to Cub is called a Negro, a colored man. Black people do not like to be called that name."

The boy's forehead wrinkled. "You mean Nigger?

"Yes".

"Why not?"'

For a minute Labounty considered the words he would use.

"Well, to them it's degrading."

Cub expressed confusion saying, "Jonathan Labounty, you surely do like usin' them big words." The boy was now back to Johnathan Labounty and seemed to have dropped Mr. Labounty. He shrugged his shoulders and apologized for his advanced vocabulary, "Sorry Cub. Degrading in this case means being called something less than you are. It's a lot like calling someone a bad name, like dumb or stupid, when in fact they're not."

"Yeah, but Nigger is all I ever heard em' called." Cub responded.

"Well trust me, not everyone calls them that, usually the ones that do are those who don't understand or just have no feelings for others. Remember, everyone, no matter what the color of their skin might be, have feelings and take pride in their heritage."

"Their what?"

"Heritage, it means legacy, birthright."

The boy shook his head, "There ya go again!"

Labounty sighed but continued. "It's a lot like these mountains. It used to be only the Indian people lived here exclusively. Then white folks like you and I came, settled, and just kept coming, more and more and more. So now, the Indian can no longer claim them as their own. The Indian people, sad to say, were driven out, at least most of them, and sent to reservations, mostly because they fought to try and keep their land".

Labounty folded Cub's blanket as he continued to talk. "You see, the white man is trying to force them to learn to live his way, but most Indians have no desire to do so. They do not want to live in towns like us and build restaurants and stores and houses. Instead, they prefer to live the way their ancestors did, close to nature. They are proud to be an Indian and want to be known as such. Their hearts are happiest when following in the ways of their father and their father's father. It's their preferred way, the Indian way. It's their birthright, their heritage."

Cub looked down at his feet, thought a minute, then looked up.

"I think I understand it. It's kind of like a Pa and his son. If the Pa was a farmer and was happy bein' a farmer, and raised his son to be a farmer, then the son will be happy to be a farmer too, just like his Pa, right?"

Labounty smiled and let it show.

"Right Cub. You're smart when you take time to think things out. I'm proud of you." Labounty ruffled his hair, and the boy returned his smile.

"Come on," Labounty told him joyfully, placing the blanket in the pack- saddle, "let's get going."

They mounted and rode on, splashing across the stream in the direction of the awaiting desert. Around them birds chirped in the scattered trees and a dawdling sun continued to pour its warmth down upon them. The air was clean and fresh, and maybe, Labounty thought, just maybe, having company wasn't such a bad thing.

CHAPTER SIX

By the time they stopped for the night a jagged patchwork of shadows had buried the timbered slopes behind them. Staring in their direction Labounty informed Cub of the importance of setting up quickly, for even as he spoke, those same shadows were swallowing the meadow and moving rapidly. In less than half an hour it would overtake them as well, and with its darkness would come a harsh night chill.

While Cub unsaddled the horses and pack mule Labounty left the site and entered a small group of trees to the north. Utilizing what little bit of light that remained he hoped for a shot at a rabbit or pheasant. It was important they save the remaining rations of Beans and Bacon for their journey across the desert.

The spot where they had made camp was the center of a small group of spruce a hundred yards from the woods where he had entered to hunt. He did not want to be too far from the boy and yet distant enough to ensure the hustle of camp did not disturb potential game.

The woods overlooked the northern half of a large meadow hosting a small, green-watered lake. Labounty hoped to spot an animal coming from or going there to quench its thirst. Inside the tree line where he moved it was already dusky and helped conceal his movement. The meadow itself remained fairly lighted by the small bit of sun left in the western sky; so, with rifle in hand he sat motionless against a tree truck, eyes scanning for movement.

Beyond the meadow the horizon lay streaked in crimson. A trace of wispy clouds stretched across the sky, and above their heads a bright full moon waited patiently for its turn to light the earth. Crickets scattered throughout the tall grass chirped their approval of the fast-approaching darkness. And as Labounty sat alone in the stillness he hoped the rumbling of his stomach would not frighten away all potential game within seeing distance.

But less than five minutes later, just a few hundred feet out, a herd of six deer crossed cautiously with a large buck sporting a rack of twelve or so points in the lead. Labounty watched him raise his head and sniff while the does stood with ears up. To shoot the buck, or one of the trailing does would have been easy. But to kill one of them for only a single meal was not to Labounty's liking, so he let them pass.

After fifteen minutes of listening to his stomach he gave up and returned to camp. Cub had the fire going and coffee over to boil. Labounty had elected to not set up the lean-too. Tonight, they would sleep in the open beneath the stars. He had reservations about even building a fire now that they were in the open meadows, but the spruce would help conceal the flames. When he walked in empty handed the youngster grinned.

"Reckon I should a done the huntin' and you set up camp."

Labounty smiled and told him to hush.

It was just as he had said, with the arrival of darkness came a noticeable chill. Together they sat huddled close to the fire wrapped in blankets. The fire flames danced to a soft wind and gentle shadows flickered across their faces. But the fire felt warm and after refilling his coffee cup Labounty decided to indulge an occasional liking. He pulled the makings from his coat pocket and built a smoke. As he lit it with a twig from the fire Cub asked.

"Mind if I have one of those?"

Labounty raised his eyebrows. "One what?"

Cub frowned.

"A smoke! You know, the thing between your fingers." Cub shook his head, "Ya know Jonathan Labounty, sometimes I wonder if maybe you have an empty noggen."

"Me too." Labounty told him with no humor in his voice. "There must be something wrong with me for worrying over you the way I do. In answer to your question, "NO, you cannot have one!"

"Well big piles of turtle turds, I swear, why in the hell not?"

Labounty shook his head. "Good Lord boy, why is it I find myself always explaining everything to you? Can't you learn that when I say no, it's no?"

"YEAH! I'm learning it real fast." Cub barked.

Shaking his head again Labounty added, "Look, I just don't think that a young boy… man, like you, should be smoking, that's all. It doesn't look natural."

"Yeah," Cub said right back, "like the way bathin' don't FEEL natural". He looked away into the darkness then and for an awkward moment remained quiet. Labounty took a sip of coffee and waited patiently, watching the youngster.

Finally, still looking away, the boy asked, "Did ya really mean what ya said about carin' for me?"

Holding his eyes on the youngster, Labounty nodded. "Yes, I did Cub."

Nothing else was said. And for an hour or longer there was silence between them. Labounty smoked and drank coffee while the boy poked at the fire and spent long spells lost in thought. Labounty wanted to say something to him but had no idea where to begin. He wanted to reach out and just hold the boy and promise him things would work out for the best, to have faith, and to trust him. But somehow, he seemed to know now was not the time.

Above their head stars were thick and twinkled in the blackness. A bright full moon sent silvery light shimmering across the meadow and crickets continued with their chirping. All around fireflies lit up the openness and it all added to the beauty of a calm mountain night; at least foothills of a Mountain night Labounty lamented.

Poking his stick at the fire and not looking up Cub suddenly asked.

"You afraid of the dark Jonathan Labounty?"

Following a glance at the boy, Labounty refilled his coffee cup. In his mind he was thinking of the proper reply. The question was something he had never been asked before and he wanted to answer correctly. So finally, with the cup filled he sat back.

"That's a good question, Cub", Labounty began, "The dark itself doesn't scare me I guess, but what sometimes can come out of it does. I know a lot of folks who fear it. They shouldn't, for darkness brings with it rest. It's a time for a tired body to recover, to recuperate from a hard day of pushing it, and too often pushing it harder than they should. Then again, for some, it's a time of superstition". He took a sip thoughtfully, adding, "Many of the Indians for instance believe that if they die at night their spirit is doomed to walk in darkness forever."

Cub's eyes raised with interest, and he looked up.

"Wow. Do you think that's true?"

"Who's to say, Cub? We believe in Heaven and Hell. Some of the people in India believe Cows are holy and worship them as their Gods. Others believe in a thing called reincarnation where the soul keeps returning to earth in a different body to live again and again, time after time so that each trip back they become a little more better person."

Cub's eyes were glued on Labounty. Somewhere in the nearby darkness a Whippoorwill began to call. Taking another sip of coffee Labounty asked the boy what he believed. The youngster shrugged thoughtfully.

"Ain't really sure, I guess. I mean, I ain't never give it much thought. Believe it or not, when I was a small boy, I used to go to church with my real folks. It ain't the best recollection, but I do recall the preacher talkin' about sinnin' an' shit… I mean stuff. But I just never gave a lot of thinkin' to things of that sort. I guess I just looked to Ma and Pa for everything. I guess kids ain't supposed to have to think about it."

Labounty smiled lightly.

"That's right, Cub. Kids are supposed to have fun and not worry about the thing's grownups have to. There will be plenty of time for that when you get older. What's important is laughing and making new friends, learning responsibility a little at a time, and growing up slowly. Don't try and become a man overnight, it's a sure way of getting cheated out of the best part of life. Believe me, this life we live is far too short and precious to waste."

Stopping there, Labounty winked at him and smiled. "You know, I think maybe that's enough talk for one night. Tomorrow will be a full day and we should be getting close to the desert. Why don't you turn in and get some sleep?"

The boy nodded and said, "Yes sir, see ya in the mornin'."

Labounty watched him curl up in his warm blanket and close his eyes. Through the trees out in the meadow the fireflies continued to glow amid the silver light. Listening to the singing of the crickets, Labounty pulled his-own blanket tight around him, laid down and closed his eyes.

High in the heavens, the bright cheerful moon looked down, smiling. And for the remainder of the night, it would sit watching over them. Thinking of Cub, Labounty smiled too. The boy had called him sir.

CHAPTER SEVEN

Why Labounty awoke he did not know, perhaps it was just time. Whatever the reason, he felt uneasy. The sky remained dark though early strands of light had begun striating through a band of gray clouds. Lying motionless he listened to the early morning sounds. Despite the surroundings appearing to be normal, a quiet instinct warned him of impending trouble.

Slowly, without moving his blanket, he reached down and pulled his gun into his hand. Two birds fluttered in the tree to his right while deeper in, a lone squirrel chattered loudly at something it was watching.

The boy was asleep, and the fire lay in a pile of cold, gray ash. The chilled morning air was cold on his face but helped clear his senses.

Then movement in the meadow to the north caught his eye. It stopped then he caught it again. There were three men, silently inching their way toward the camp, moving first one then the other, at a distance of ten or fifteen feet apart. They were progressing slowly, probably timing it to be in position when good light arrived.

With slow careful movement Labounty nudged Cub's side with his boot toe. When the boy was awake and beginning to stir, he whispered to him quickly, "Don't move and don't say anything, just listen. In the meadow are three men moving toward us. I think they may be Paiute. Probably a small war party."

If there was fear in the boy's voice, he didn't catch it. In a low tone the youngster asked, "What are we gonna' do?"

"I'm not sure." Labounty whispered back. "When the shooting starts stay low and crawl for cover behind the tree to your left." Anger jumped into the young boy's voice then and he whispered harshly. "Runny shit and squeaky farts, Jonathan Labounty, I told ya I should have a gun. But NOOO, I'm just a little baby and can't have one."

"Shut up." Labounty, whispered sternly. "This is no time to be arguing, they'll be on us any minute."

Then the sun broke through the clouds and the war cry pierced their ears. Rolling onto his stomach Labounty fired twice and saw one of them fall. The remaining two spread out but kept coming on, yelling and firing their rifles as they moved. Bullets whizzed past Labounty, and he fired again. Another dropped but crawled behind a bush to safety. A bullet tore through Labounty's sleeve, and he cursed. Behind him came more war cries and he turned to see two more braves running onto them firing like the others. Out of the corner of his eye he caught a glimpse of Cub crawling behind the packsaddle and pile of gear, and not the tree like he'd been told. Now bullets were everywhere, he could hear them zing past his head and impacting the ground, kicking up dirt. Labounty cursed again, "Shit!"

Cub screamed at Labounty, "Look out, behind you!" Rolling on to his back Labounty fired point blank and the last warrior from the meadow collapsed in a sliding heap, tearing through the remains of the cold fire. Gray ash flew up in a flurry of dust. Rifle fire echoed endlessly through the open meadow. The two behind Labounty were covering the ground fast. So, rolling over three times he remained on his back and fired another round. It missed and he didn't get a chance for another- they were on top of him now and it was hand-to-hand. One he kicked and heard groan as he rolled to the side curled in a ball. The other was strong, and it was all Labounty could do to hold the wrist with the knife pointed down at his face.

Teeth gritted, Labounty struggled against the Indians' power, knowing that any second the other would recover and when he did, it would be all but over. The ground on which they fought was wet with morning dampness.

Then suddenly something was shouted in Paiute and Labounty recognized the word to mean, STOP. If that wasn't enough, the rifle barrel that suddenly appeared pointed at his head was overwhelmingly convincing; all struggling ceased.

The warrior he had been fighting scrambled to his feet and he along with the one holding the rifle exchanged a quick run of conversation in their language. There was a short burst of laughter between them, and their eyes along with Labounty's, slowly turned to Cub.

The boy was standing on his feet behind the packsaddle, his face white with fear. In his hands he held a pistol, cocked and pointed at the chest of the warrior with the rifle. His little hands were shaking but he never blinked an eye. At first the two standing braves looked unsure. Then, after a few seconds they glanced at one another and started laughing again. Labounty wanted to make a move, but the rifle was too far away and still pointed at his head. The brave who he had been struggling with, grinned at Cub then spoke to him in broken English.

"Put gun down, you, papoose not man. You no even have muscle to pull trigger."

Cub's white face turned red with anger.

"Who you callin' a baby you red-skinned puke breath?"

The warrior's face went sober for a minute while he tried to figure out what the boy had said. Cub didn't wait and went on to say, "Tell your twin butt cheek there to drop the rifle or I'm gonna' shoot him in his tracks."

Again, there was a moment of confused expression on the Indian's face. The one Cub was talking with turned to the warrior with the rifle and spoke to him in Paiute. The barrel pulled away a little but still they were too far for Labounty to successfully make a move. The two talked for a brief period, their voices rising in tone. Apparently, they figured they had better start taking the boy seriously. Pointing a finger finally, the interpreter said, "You put down gun and we no kill you."

"That's a big pile a shit!" Cub replied. "Tell him to drop the rifle or I'll shoot him in the chest and you through the balls."

That struck a nerve and was clearly interpreted. They started jabbering like a couple of old women.

It was obvious the one holding the rifle was angered; with speed that streaked in a blur the Indian pulled the barrel around to Cub and would fire long before Labounty could reach him. There was no time left for Cub to try and reason, the moment of truth had come… instinct or die.

The slug from the Winchester would tear through his little body like paper if he did not pull the trigger now. From Labounty's mouth came the scream that felt an eternity in getting out. The boy did not realize a rifle slug at that range would take half his back.

"SHOOT, CUB!" From Labounty it was a scream!

The big gun kicked wildly in his little hands. Smoke belched from the barrel and the sound of the bullet leaving the muzzle screamed across the open meadow. The recoil knocked Cub backwards while the bullet that struck the Indian sent him flying backwards too, sprawling onto his back dead before his body quit moving.

Instantly tackling the standing warrior, Labounty was once again in a struggle for his life. Slamming hard to the ground they rolled over twice. The warrior's right hand came up with a knife while his left gripped Labounty's throat. The blade was close, and he was easily equal in strength.

Labounty threw a roundhouse to the Indian's temple, and he cried out in pain. Then he gave him another, and still yet another. The Indian groaned but didn't budge. This warrior was considerably bigger in body-mass than Labounty. The blade inched closer.

Labounty was quickly realizing he misjudged, the man he fought was not his equal, but rather, this enemy was the stronger. Labounty's breath was nearly choked out of him as the warrior's powerful squeeze slowly crushed his neck; blood gorged the veins in his head and his face had turned red, he knew there was no way he could win. The blade of the knife dropped within an inch of his chest. There was no holding him, in seconds the sharp steel would be plunging into his heart.

Then Cub was there suddenly with the big gun still in his hands. He stuck the barrel in the warrior's face and yelled for him to stop. And that's just what the big Indian did. Fighting for breath both men slowly climbed to their feet.

"Drop the knife." Cub spoke the words with a tone that said he was not going to negotiate this time. The big Indian obeyed without hesitation. The knife fell onto the ground beside him and Labounty kicked it away.

This time the boy's hands were not shaking. He looked sternly into the Indian's face, gun ready and pointed.

"Out in that meadow," Cub said, "there's one of your kind, he's hurt. Go help him and get out of here. And stay gone. You come back and I'll do what I done promised."

The Indian paused a moment, deciphering Cub's words. Suddenly, across his face there came an expression of enlightenment and he looked down at his crotch, then back at Cub. He said something in his own tongue then raised his hands and backed away slowly.

They watched him walk out into the meadow to where the wounded Indian lay. Helping him to his feet they ambled awkwardly out of sight in the direction of the lake.

Labounty turned to Cub and for a long time they stared. Their eyes were locked and faces without expression. What was there to say? Cub had saved his life. Taking the gun from his hands, Labounty took him in his arms and hugged him.

"You know," he said proudly, "there's an old saying, 'never judge a book by its cover.' I owe you my life little man. THANKS."

Cub smiled at him then and it was a warm smile. A smile that came from his heart but one that also said… 'You're welcome, but I told you so'. After breaking camp, they rode away, leaving the Indian bodies where they had fallen. Their comrades would care for them in their own way. Labounty knew the boy had killed his first man and in his heart he would be troubled. When the youngster was ready and wanted to talk about it, Labounty would be there to listen.

CHAPTER EIGHT

The remaining journey to Yuma would be challenging and they would need to travel with extreme caution. Whether or not Paiute would pursue them Labounty did not know, but they would need to be ready if they did. By tomorrow evening they would enter the great basin below and begin the long trek across the Mojave. The Paiute would not follow them there, that was the good side, the bad side was, Labounty was not looking forward to the desert segment of the ride, and long before its end both he and the boy would be very glad to see Yuma.

Just after noon they came upon another lake and let the horse's drink. Unlike the larger lake where they had camped, this water was as blue as the sky and smooth as the face of a porcelain plate. Over their heads a Hawk soared past, casting down a long shadow as it glided low across the bank. In its claws it carried a fish, and they watched the bird with admiration.

What a feeling it would be, Labounty thought, to fly through the clouds so free. Then as if it had come out of nowhere a huge eagle appeared and soared straight to the Hawk where it began circling the smaller bird with grace, ease and a given determination.

Labounty knew well what was going to happen. There was to be a confrontation, a no contest of surrendering food or a fight to the end for the spoils. Cub was about to witness one of nature's hardest rules, survival of the fittest.

One moment the two birds were far out and seemed like only black specs against the blue backdrop, then they were near again. So near in fact, they could easily see the beautiful white head and tail feathers of the great Bald Eagle.

The Hawk cried out and its' screech skipped across the open face of the lake. Mesmerized, Cub watched the Eagle close in on the Hawk, closer and closer, until finally accepting the inevitable, the Hawk dropped its catch toward the water and flew away.

The eagle, spreading its enormous wings pitched to the right and dove with great speed catching the falling fish in its razor claws. Cub's eyes were still watching when he said excitedly, "Wow! Did you see that?"

"I sure did." Labounty said with a smile. "Guess we'd have to say the great Bald Eagle is king of the sky, you agree?"

"You can bet a pair of big titties, I…"

Quickly Cub's head came around and he looked at Labounty.

"Sorry."

Shaking his head, Labounty reined his horse away from the water's edge looking up into the blue sky and whispered it once more, "Why me?"

They traveled the remainder of the day in what was mostly silence. Always the scenery was colorful. The trees smelled of fresh pine and from the countless flowers growing in the fields, their drifted an occasional scent upon the same soft breeze that cooled them in the warm sun.

While descending a steep slope an old porcupine ambled across their path at a pace a turtle would have envied. Stopping, they let him pass. At first Cub was panicky, fearing the old porky might spray them with quills, but Labounty assured him that was not the case.

"They don't actually shoot quills," he told him, "You have to be near enough to be stabbed".

Cub looked at Labounty, "You mean ya gotta be pesterin' him before he'll send his quills a flyin'?"

Labounty nodded. "Yes, that's right. There's a good lesson to be learned from our little friend there," Labounty said, "He's like a lot of the men you'll meet in your life. He has that look that says if you don't want to get hurt, leave me alone and keep your distance."

Cub mulled the words around in his head then nodded and they rode on. And for the remainder of the day the boy pondered not only what he had just been told, but also all the other things that had been said and experienced since his meeting up with the man called Jonathan Labounty; a man he was really beginning to like.

CHAPTER NINE

They made camp when the shadows of evening began dimming the distance ahead. This night there would be no fire. If the war party were following, he did not wish to make it easy to find them.

So, for supper they ate hardtack and washed it down with water from the canteens. They had picket-penned the horses very near and made their beds within a tight group of trees that overlooked a steep slope to the front and was bordered all the way around by brush. The only quiet way in would be up the steep grade to the front and they would each take turns standing guard there. To some degree Labounty trusted the boy now, and felt he understood the serious consequences of not being careful.

He built a smoke but lit it with a cupped hand to conceal the flame of the match. The black sky was full of stars. For the first few hours of darkness, they sat together at the crest of the slope staring into the blackness below. The previous night's full moon was back and hung in good spirits as Cub sat pointing out the big dipper. It was inverted and at first difficult to spot.

"Ya know," Cub said in a quiet voice, "whenever that dipper is upside down it's a sign it's gonna' rain."

Staring at the constellation Labounty considered Cub's words.

"Well, I'm not sure how factual that is but I suppose there could be some truth to it."

"No really," the boy went on, "it happens every time I see it that way." He paused for a minute then added, "Tell ya what, I'll wager a bet with ya. Since your doubtin' and I'm not, we'll just see who's right come tomorrow."

"OK," Labounty smiled, "but what do we put up for stakes?"

He couldn't see the boy's face but was willing to bet it had a thoughtful expression.

"How about this," Cub said following a few seconds of thinking, "if you lose you can't say a word about my language for two days runnin'."

"And if I win?" Labounty asked.

"Then for two days you get to wipe my mouth out with soap every time I slip, and I won't put up a fight. Fair enough?"

"Fair enough", Labounty said, "but you know, if I win, I'll probably run out of soap before we get to Yuma."

Cub smiled into the night. "Well, if ya do, at least I won't have to stop talkin' in a way that ain't natural."

Around eleven Labounty sent Cub to bed while he took the first watch. Alone, he stared into the stars pondering the awkward hand fate had dealt him. So much had happened in the last two days. Never would he have guessed he'd become the guardian of a small boy. Yuma was far away, yet although he refused to dwell on it, it was in some ways, not far enough.

One more day and night would put them squarely in the Mesa. First, travel there would be enjoyable with breathtaking scenery and welcomed shade from tall cliffs and steeping plateaus. But in a short time, Hell itself would open its doors and they would ride into a Terra Firma of unbearable heat. A hot scorching sun would parch their lips while dust and alkali caked their clothing. Food would be scarce and water even more so.

He made a face and sighed into the night. Off in the distance he heard an all too familiar rumble and straight in front of him a single flash of lightning streaked the sky. Looking up into the heavens Labounty located the big dipper, it was still inverted the way Cub had spotted it. Another flash of lightning wiped through the blackness, but closer this time. Shaking his head, Labounty glanced back at the sleeping boy and shook his head.

Less than twenty minutes from his glancing at him, a sudden downpour woke Cub from a sound sleep. Pulling himself into a sitting position he grinned speaking above the hammering rain, "See, I told ya so. You can keep that soap packed away!"

CHAPTER TEN

Rain showers continued off and on through the night, so Labounty had given his slicker to Cub, let him sleep and he took all night watch. Come morning, they broke camp at first light and rode out into a chilly light drizzle of rain.

By noon it was gone, the sun had come out with its punishing rays and continued to grow from hot to merciless, returning the damp Mojave floor to its dry and cracked earth. The desert was now the challenge. Thick timbered slopes, sweeping meadows with blue and green water lakes, tall grass, and paddocks of colored flowers were now behind them and both somberly shared their saddles with melancholy. Gone too were soft breezes, abundant water, and treasured shade.

The remaining ride to Yuma had now become a monotonous and dangerous journey. Hour after boring hour the horses lumbered along in the horrid heat, one hoof step after the other, sweat, and alkaline caking their bodies while minds ached for the want of wet sips of water.

The slow early fall of night did finally come, bringing with it the welcomed relief of cool evening air; but also, the stark realization a cold shivering night was to follow.

The world around them now lay an expansive tableland stretching as far as the eye could see. Evening had brought with it an orange sun nestled in a sky of copper, its perfect roundness resting presumptuous upon the far edge of this desolate land.

Labounty knew they needed to travel east to reach the Colorado River. Once there they would turn south and follow it straight into Yuma. Halting his horse, he reined around so that his left side faced the setting sun. He then raised his left arm straight out from his side with his palm open, fingers pointed to the sky.

Cub pulled up alongside, thankful for a chance to stop. He was growing tired and bored from the monotonous walk of his horse. Yawning, he watched Labounty curiously then asked.

"What in Hellfire ya doin'?"

Frowning, Labounty looked at him. "Cub, I know you won the bet with the rain, and I know I'm not supposed to say anything, but do you have to use that language all the time?"

Now Cub frowned, "Well cry like a spanked baby, why don't ya. Your actin' like you're some kinda' preacher or somethin". A man outta be talkin' the way it feels natural."

"No," Labounty cut in, "talking the way you should, and talking the way you think you should, are two separate things. You don't hear me talking that way all the time, now do you?"

"No."

"Well then, do as I do."

The boy was quiet then, thinking over what he had just been told.

Labounty spoke again, this time answering the boy's question. "What I am doing is finding the correct direction we need to go. It's an old Indian way for finding north and south. You see the way my chest is facing?"

"Yeah."

"Well, that way is north. We need to go east so it is simply a matter of turning accordingly. The trick is, in the morning you use your right hand pointed to the sun, and in the afternoon your left; forget that rule and you could end up lost or dead. Understand?"

Cub nodded thoughtfully. "Yep."

Reining his horse around and pretending not to see, Labounty smiled as he caught a glimpse of Cub raising his arm to the sun.

By seven it was dark, and they made camp along the bank of an old riverbed. After building a small fire of twisted cedar limbs they sat back and relaxed.

Labounty did not make coffee. He certainly would have liked a cup, but until they reached Colorado River, water would be rationed with caution. So, for supper they ate hardtack again chased with only a swallow of the wet stuff. When finished, Labounty rolled a smoke and lay back against his saddle.

He looked over at the boy sitting near the fire. His blanket was wrapped around his shoulders, and he was staring intently into the flames. Taking a long draw on his cigarette Labounty gave the youngster thought. He really was a good kid. The boy had just fallen victim to his environment; having spent much too long a time with the men he had found him with; influenced by their manners, or their lack thereof.

Cub had no idea how to be a young boy or that it was even fun for that matter. All he had had time for was surviving, merely living from day to day. It was not fair, and he deserved better. The boy deserved at least a chance at a good life; an education, friends, home, and some form of parental love.

Somewhere beyond the fire a coyote called into the night and Labounty shifted his thinking. Resting his head against the saddle seat he looked up into the night sky. A million stars glittered like twinkling candles and a near full moon cast soothing light around them. The fire flames radiated comforting warmth and, in his soul, Labounty felt peace, the kind of peace that comes from the company of another. Tossing his cigarette into the moonlit desert he looked once again at the boy.

"Hey Cub."

The youngster replied without looking up, fixated on the fire flames dancing to the soft crackle of burning wood.

"Yeah?"

"I was wondering. How was it you got hooked up with the likes of those men I found you with?"

Shrugging his shoulders but never taking his eyes from the fire, the boy told him.

"About four or so years ago, Pa and I were in El Paso. He was there lookin' into work. I don't recall what kind. One night we was out walkin', just sort a takin' in the sights when we heard a bunch a shootin' from across the street. It was comin' from one of the saloons."

Cub paused and cleared his throat. "It all happened so fast. Two men come runnin' out of the saloon backwards, shootin' as they came out. Pa grabbed me, I suspect to protect me." The boy paused again and took a deep breath. He started to speak again but paused a third time. A minute or so went by, then clearing his throat again and continued. "Anyway, three other men come out of the doors shootin' at the other two. Bullets were hitting all around us everywhere. And two of them hit…"

His voice caught in his throat and the firelight reflected the tears welling in his eyes, but he continued, "Two of the bullets hit Pa and killed him."

Cub broke into tears then and began crying aloud. Moving to his side, Labounty took him in his arms and held him gently. Searching for words, he could find none that felt right so instead of speaking, he just held the boy close. He guessed this was probably a well overdue cry that Cub had been holding inside for a long while.

For several minutes the boy whimpered, and he held him, never loosening his hug. And as he held him, Labounty stared up into the sky at the stars; there were still just as many, and they shined bright as ever; but their glittering splendor did not ease the pain. Hurting inside himself, he sat quietly, wishing he could have been there with the boy and his father. Maybe he could have helped.

A long while they sat huddled together, silhouetted by the firelight; the man holding the boy. And out in the darkness, far away, the lone coyote called out again, but this time another answered. And in his heart Labounty blinked his eyes. At least not everyone was alone in this world.

After Cub had had his cry, he pulled away and stared off into the darkness. Wiping his eyes with his sleeve he told Labounty. "You think I'm some kinda sissy now, don't ya? Since I cried!"

Labounty searched carefully for the proper words. "I think you're more of a man than some grown men I know, Cub. You should never be ashamed to show your feelings. That's why the good Lord gave them to us. You earned that cry and you deserved to have it. It's important to get things off your chest. I know you want very much to be a man, but you must realize there is a difference between acting like a man and trying to act like a man". Labounty hesitated, again choosing his words carefully. "Cub, I do not care how big or small you are, there's a time for laughing, a time for being serious and a time for crying. Yours was a time for crying and I am not a bit ashamed of you. In fact, it impressed me."

Looking up into Labounty's eyes, Cub grew serious, relieved that he hadn't acted like a big baby after all.

"I impressed you?" He asked.

"Why sure". Labounty went on. "Anybody can hold their feelings inside, that is easy. But not everyone is grown up enough to let them out, to let them show, especially around other people. That takes courage. And lately, you sure have been showing me you're a young man with plenty of courage."

Labounty gave the boy one more hug and returned to his place at his saddle. Cub watched him return then said. "I'd like to finish telling you now if it's alright."

Labounty nodded silently and the youngster continued.

"After Pa was killed, them three you found me with, took me in. They weren't exactly royalty, but they were all I had. All that is except for Uncle Pete and Aunt Gladys in…"

He made a face, mumbled under his breath but continued. "In Yuma! Anyhow, I traveled with Red and them until that night they tried to kill ya."

"What about your mother?" Labounty asked.

"Ma died when I was six. Real bad fever." Suddenly Cub smiled. "She sure was pretty, Mr. Labounty. And she could sing like an angel come down from Heaven. Every night she would read to me from the Bible and tell me stories. Back then Pa was a rancher, and we'd go to church every Sunday mornin'."

His eyes lit up and he smiled wider. "Ma was in the choir you know. She used to wear this really pretty robe of yellow. And boy, could she cook. Sometimes after eatin' Ma's Sunday dinner, Pa and I would bet on who was the fullest, and we'd pull up our shirts and see who had the biggest belly. Ma used to really get onto us about that."

His face went sober. "When Ma died it was hard on both Pa and me, especially Pa, I think? He began losin' interest in the ranch and after a couple years he sold it and we moved to Texas. Pa spent quite a lot of time there movin' from job to job. Then one day he got to readin' the paper and before I knew it, we were heading for El Paso". Cub glanced at Labounty, "I told you the rest."

The youngster started to say something else but instead caught himself and rose to his feet. "Well, Mr. Labounty," he said without looking at him, "I'm pretty tired. Reckon I'll turn in."

Labounty watched him walk to his bedroll and curl up. The boy was troubled, and it made Labounty feel helpless. He knew the youngster disliked the idea of going to Yuma, of having to live with his aunt and uncle. But based on his life prior to the mountain men and once he got a fresh taste of decent living again, he'd be much happier than he was now. And eventually he would come to realize it.

Times were changing; it was getting harder for a man to find work. Cattle drives were slowly becoming a thing of the past with a large percentage of cattle being shipped by rail. People were living in most every part of the country and new machines were taking the place of honest, hardworking men.

There was even talk of the horseless carriage one day taking the place of the horse itself. And with such a change the need for a good education would come to be. If Cub was to survive, education was what he needed. This was a bad way of life for a small boy. He needed a family, a lovely home, and at least a semblance of a mother and father. Taking him to Yuma was the right thing to do. Surely it was. It had to be!

CHAPTER ELEVEN

The two kneeling men were holding the woman's wrists so tight her hands had begun to grow numb. She lay upon her back poked and scratched by scores of tiny stones. She had not screamed though, as the men had expected. In fact, so far, she had not even fought them.

A third man, tall, hair to his shoulders and broad across the chest, stood towering at her feet. One button at a time he was undoing his shirt, the smirk on his gruff whiskered face telling of his total lack of compassion for her. What he was about to do was going to cause her pain, but that did not matter to him. The only thing of consequence was that he was getting what he wanted.

In silence the woman glared straight into his eyes with cold contempt. Though she lay inert, hatred raged, and revenge boiled resentfully in her heart. And if she had a pistol he would have already been in pain, bleeding and missing a major body part.

Across the desert the hot sun sent heat waves dancing above the baked earth, creating a lonely land of deceiving mirages. And that's what Labounty thought he saw; that is until he and the boy rode closer. The three men were so intent upon what they were doing they had not noticed the two approaching.

Only a few feet away Cub and Labounty halted their Horses side by side, sitting their saddles and making no sound. The boy's eyes were big with disbelief and youthful curiosity. Labounty was concerned for him. Inevitably there would be a fight and by the time they had come upon the men and woman, it had been too late to turn the boy away.

With careful eyes Labounty studied the three men. All wore guns, but only the one standing wore it low. He would be the one to watch closely. This man was tall with shoulder length hair and pushing the high side of thirty or so. He was broad across the shoulders and if Labounty's guess was right, this one would be confident and sure of himself.

As for the two kneeling men, one was short, balding, and horse-big around the belly. The other was tall and lanky with an honest Abe kind of look. However, Labounty was reasonably sure this man was not presidential material. All three needed shaves and had obviously been riding hard for some time.

Slowly, Labounty slipped the field strap free from the hammer of his pistol; he would have preferred pulling his rifle from its scabbard, but there had not been time and to draw it now could prove a fatal mistake. The sun was hot on his back, and he felt a bead of sweat race downward between his shoulder blades.

The woman they held looked to be in her mid-thirties, possibly early forties. What she was doing in the middle of the Mohave was a puzzling question. If it had been the men who brought her here, they intended to do more than just have their way; she was marked for a bullet. No better place existed for killing someone and not having to worry over the remains being found.

Labounty's eyes swept her quickly. She was strikingly beautiful with long hair the color of a copper sunset. It lay gathered on the ground beneath her, and he guessed it would hang in the middle of her back when standing. A light blue calico dress trimmed with white lace had been pulled up to her waist with her pantaloon's torn free from her body and thrown to the side. She was petite, perhaps five six or seven with milky white skin turning red from too much exposure to the desert sun. There was nothing from which to judge her character. She was dressed nicely, clean, smooth skin that had been well cared for over the years, and she was not fighting the men like a frightened schoolgirl would; and it wasn't because she didn't mind what these animals were doing.

This woman, Labounty guessed, did not come from a western cow town saloon. On the contrary, the sense one sometimes gets told him this woman was a lady, a gentlewoman, kind and self-assured. Labounty took a deep breath. Regardless of who or what she was it did not matter, now, she was extremely helpless and in great danger.

Labounty could feel his anger mounting. What these cowboys were doing he considered the worst atrocity imaginable by man. And it certainly was nothing the boy should be seeing.

The woman herself was the first to notice the two. Initially she saw only the horses and that two men sat atop them. But closer observation revealed one was but a small boy. Her eyes moved from Cub to Labounty, and the two stared.

Even with the distance between them, she could see his disdain for the filth taking their liberties. This was not his fight she knew, but somehow understood with a sense of thankfulness he was about to make it so. In line with her appreciation, concern for him out shadowed her-own misfortune, and equally, she worried for the boy. Death lingered around them, and she silently prayed it would not be this man or the child.

It was the one standing that first realized someone was present, for the woman was staring intently over his shoulder. Doing that which a smart man would do, he lowered his hands from the buttons of his shirt to his gun. Then slowly, carefully, almost mechanically he turned until finally he stood facing Labounty.

As he turned his first sight was that of the boy, so when his eyes fell upon Labounty he smiled confidently. He liked the odds, one man and a helpless kid against three guns.

There was unspoken tension in the air as both men sized up the other. The sky above was rich with blue and white and around them the hot desert waited. Labounty spoke his words coldly first, then edged them with a scorn he did not try and hide.

"Having a little filthy fun, are we?"

The standing man, whose hand was now at his gun, held his smile and replied. "Well stranger," his eyes darted to Cub then back, "or should I say stranger and runt."

Immediately Cub rose in his saddle red in the face. "Who in hell you callin' a runt, buffalo shit?"

Not removing his eyes from the standing man, Labounty cut in. "Cub, shut up."

The standing man's tone came with warning.

"You and your smart-mouthed son better turn around and ride away right now."

The two kneeling men released the woman's hands and rose to their feet. Unsure herself of the situation, the woman remained where she was.

Labounty did not like the odds but to turn and ride away now, leaving the woman behind, would put him on the same level as the three men he faced.

"No mister," Labounty said, "we're not going anywhere. But I'll tell you what. You leave the lady with us, then the boy and I will let the three of you ride out unharmed, that sound fair?"

The man's smile returned. He began to laugh out loud. And in the middle of his laughter, he went for his gun. The other two men followed instinctively. At that same instant, the woman, still on the ground, kicked out with her right leg and caught the big man with the unbuttoned shirt in the groin. Her intent was to cripple him forever.

Yelling painfully into the desert heat, he grabbed his groin and crumbled to his knees. Above his yell was heard two shots- so close together that to an inexperienced ear they may have sounded as one.

The two men who had been holding the woman's wrists, one with his gun falling from his hand, and the other with it still half in its holster, fell together following the roar of Labounty's 44; one was dead instantly and the other twitched as the last breath of life left his body.

Labounty re-holstered his weapon with noticeable grace and speed equal to his draw. Cub sat staring, astonished just how fast he had both drawn and fired.

"Wow Jonathan Labounty," Cub said in amazement, "you're fast." Ignoring the boy's remark Labounty swung down from the saddle and approached the woman who had climbed to her feet and was brushing off her dress.

"Thank you," Labounty told her smiling, "you probably saved my life."

Halting her brushing she looked into his eyes and returned the smile. "No, it is me who owes you the thanks. Besides, kicking that animal was pure pleasure."

Labounty stuck out his hand and she took it. Her touch was soft.

"I'm Johnathan Labounty."

"Kay. Kay Martin." She replied, widening her smile continuing to hold onto his hand.

They stared for a few awkward seconds, and she released it. Then together turned and looked down on the man she had kicked. Still on his knees, he held his arms about his mid-section, seeming a little less in pain. His gun lay on the ground in front of him, so Labounty picked it up, tucking it in his belt.

The sun above their heads was blistering, its vile heat lingering. Cub dismounted with his canteen and took it to the woman. Gratefully she accepted it and told him what a nice little boy he was. Labounty smiled and Cub frowned at him. Looking straight into the woman's face Cub informed he sternly, but politely, "Ma'am, I'm not a little boy, so please don't ever call me that again. I'm a man, just ask Mr. Labounty."

Surprised, the woman named Kay looked to Labounty for clarity. Labounty glanced down at Cub and told her. "He is just that Ms Martin, a little big man." This time Cub nodded his approval with a smile.

After stripping the unneeded horses of all gear, they turned them loose. The canteens, food and ammunition Labounty transferred to the pack mule and made ready to move on. He bound the hands of the cowboy the woman had kicked, then sat him in his saddle and tied his legs beneath the horse's belly for security.

Of the extra horses, he retained a blue roan with white socks for the woman, choosing that animal for two reasons. First, it was strong and spirited, and secondly, the woman had considered him the prettiest of the lot. The second reason was not one he considered a priority for choosing him. However, out of good judgment, Labounty kept that opinion to himself.

After burying the two dead men beneath rocks and brush they rode out.

The sun remained hot, but the heat waves had thinned, and a slight coolness could be felt in the air. Another three hours and night would cover the wasteland once again. Labounty decided they would travel well into the dark hours in hopes of reaching the river by nightfall of the following day. He had not figured on the extra riders, especially one bound and the other a woman, but there was no need in complaining over what had to be. As the horses sauntered along, he gave thought to the situation.

The gunman would have to be watched every minute until they reached Yuma. There he would turn him over to the sheriff; the man would go to prison no doubt, and deservingly so. As for the woman, he knew nothing about her; where she came from, what she was doing here, or where she had been headed. With a side glance he studied her.

His guess about the hair had been accurate; it flowed full-length to the midsection of her back. And despite the searing rays of sun burning her skin, the redness somehow gave compliment. Her lips had begun showing signs of cracking and he knew they pained her; yet she sat her horse with dignity and never complained. He admired her spirit. The fact that she was beautiful he could not deny. The dress she wore had obviously been tailored to fit, and while it did not flaunt her wares, it did highlight the fact she was a woman. Earlier when she had smiled, he noticed the striking whiteness of her teeth, and when she had taken his hand the softness of her touch. She was a woman of class and likely educated. Of all the things that made her a woman, it had been her grace that stood out most. And while her brown eyes were notably lovely, it was the mystery behind them that intrigued him.

Turning back around Labounty built a smoke. Striking his match, he lit the cigarette and inhaled deeply. What did it matter anyway he thought, when they reached Yuma he would turn the tied man over to the sheriff, walk Kay Martin to the Hotel, ensure she had a room and say good-by. Then take Cub to his Aunt and Uncle. Once done; he would return to the Mountains.

Looking off into the desert he made a face and pondered: a man could be the judge of a good horse, count on the faithfulness of his dog, shoot a rifle true to its mark, and hope at the end of the cowboy's final ride he would face the Maker with confidence. However, regarding women… only one thing did any man know - a woman was a woman.

CHAPTER TWELVE

hey rode the entire day single file and quiet. The sun drained their strength, weakened their will and warmed the canteens to a detestable degree. Through each long-drawn hour, they thought of shade and sleep.

By eight that night they had stopped and set up a temporary camp. The woman put over a pot of coffee from the extra water they now possessed and warmed some beans. Total darkness had not yet come, but a light dusk was settling in, and a welcomed coolness refreshed their tired bodies.

The bound stranger remained discreet for the most part, speaking very little. All that Labounty knew of him at this point was that he went by the name of Bracewell. Several times he had caught the man watching the trail behind and doing so in a manner not to be noticed. Labounty remained watchful.

After throwing a small cedar limb onto the fire, he left the others and walked to a spot where he could watch over the trail from which they had come. Sitting, he laid his rifle across his lap and began thinking.

As far as he knew the gunman's friends were dead, and there had been no sign of any others. Watching their trail through the day there had been no indication they were being followed. Yet, he had to admit that if there was someone out there, they could be men who knew what they were doing, and he could be significantly outnumbered.

After rolling a cigarette he lit it then leaned back on an elbow. It was growing darker now and shadows lay thick around them. Only a few stars showed in the sky and a partial moon hung hiding behind clouds. The air was cool and the urge, or warning, to saddle up and ride filled him with uneasiness.

Taking a draw from his cigarette he sighed. Three more days and they would be in Yuma. There he could rest easily and catch up on the needed sleep. Glancing back toward the fire he studied the three figures sitting around it.

Cub picked at his beans distastefully, worried about making it to Yuma. Twice he had caught the boy talking with Bracewell and broke it up. The youngster was ready to run, and he certainly did not need Bracewell edging him on. If he did take off, Labounty could only hope the boy wouldn't try it here. If he did, it could prove a major problem with a woman and a prisoner to watch while tracking him.

The woman's condition was worsening. From reflection of the firelight, he could tell she was burned badly despite her brave front. Her lips were beginning to blister and that was in addition to the dried cracks. She was hurting and he knew it. Her fair skin was just no match for the desert sun. But she did have spirit and that was a good part of what it took to survive the odds.

Bracewell was the real problem. He was undoubtedly a killer and had to be watched closely. Like Cub he had no intention of making it to Yuma. And unlike the boy he would stop short of nothing in escaping, even killing, regardless of whom.

Labounty shook his head and looked back up into the night sky. The moon was free of the clouds and now shining brightly. He could see its face, its darkened eyes and nose and it seemed to be smiling; perhaps it knew something he didn't. It was a near full moon and a beautiful one, peaceful and far away.

The woman appeared suddenly beside him holding two cups of coffee. Pulling himself into a sitting position, Labounty took one of the cups appreciatively.

"Thanks."

Kay Martin sat beside him and together they turned to look out into the open desert. For what seemed a long while they sat without speaking. Labounty counted sixteen stars in the sky, and twice the moon disappeared behind drifting clouds of dark gray. The air was chilly, and he was thankful, for it would help keep him awake while on watch.

To their backs the fire burned low and the distant warmth from the flames did little in fighting the nippy air surrounding them. The open country was quiet, and they heard only the crackling of the fire and their own breathing. Then the woman turned to look at him. She was close, and while it made him nervous, he liked the feel of it too.

"I want to thank you again Mr. Labounty for what you did for me today. Who knows what might have become of me had you not come to my rescue. I'm quite sure once finished, they would have killed me."

Labounty took a sip of his coffee. Although he agreed, he did not say so and said instead, "Kill you? That's strong."

"I know it sounds melodramatic, but please, allow me to tell you everything. I suspect you're wondering what I'm doing out here in this God forsaken country in the first place."

Labounty nodded. "I guess I am."

"Less than a month ago I lived in Chicago. I own and manage a large Hotel there." She paused and took a sip of coffee. "Three Saturdays ago, I attended a party given by a banker friend of mine, or at least I believed him to be a friend. At the party his son Charles, a twenty-one-year-old, and if I may use the term in your presence, a pompous ass, began to…" She paused, looked away and took another sip of coffee. "Halfway into the evening and with more than his share of whisky under his belt,

Charles began coming around, acting as though I were his date… more like personal property actually. He asked me to dance and of course out of respect for his father, I accepted. But as we danced his hands began showing up on parts of my body where they did not belong. It became a struggle just to maintain my dignity. People were staring and pointing, and the young man was far too drunk to care. As embarrassing as it was, there was no averting his hands, I suspect one could compare it to wrestling with an octopus during its need to mate."

Labounty laughed at her description, and she turned to look at him with a stern expression.

"Do you find a woman being pawed in public humorous, Mr. Labounty? It happened to have caused me an unbearable amount of embarrassment, not to mention problems you can't imagine."

Labounty apologized. "No, certainly not Ms. Martin, I wasn't laughing at you. I was just…"

Angry, she cut in, "You weren't laughing at me, you were just thinking out loud, right? Labounty puckered his lips thinking, here we go, the molehill becoming a mountain. 'Well, let me tell you Mr. Labounty, you're wrong. The problem is much more serious than that."

"Look", Labounty injected, "I didn't mean anything by laughing. I just…"

"I know. You just wanted to assure me it was nothing more than a young man just being a young man?"

Labounty started to say something again, but she stopped him by climbing to her feet and glaring down. "I should have known better than to expect a man to understand. Sometimes I think you are all cut from the same stretch of cowhide".

Turning, she stormed back to the fire. Exasperated, Labounty watched her go, wondering what had just happened. The moon came out from behind a cloud spilling silvery light. Kay Martin walked to the far side of the fire and plopped down hard on the ground; her face angry. Turning back around, Labounty stared out into the open desert gulping down the remainder of his coffee. One word soft as a whisper came out of his mouth… "WOMEN!"

By eleven they were back in the saddle and pushing again. The night air was growing colder and Labounty navigated by the stars. The pallid moon draped the desert in dim ashen light and more stars came out glittering like distant candles. Around them the shadows of night lay gathered, mystic and secret. Hour after long hour passed.

In their saddles they slept, heads bowed, and bodies limber. Throughout the night lone coyotes called, howling at this quiet and lonely land, a world of strange and bizarre shapes altered by the dark of night, radiant moon and endless fringes of the imagination.

CHAPTER THIRTEEN

They strolled through the night rocking restlessly in the saddle. Stunted Pinion trees now stretched across the parched desert floor and the ungodly heat persisted. Its rays continued to burn cruel and vicious, blistering and reddening any exposed skin, dehydrating their bodies to a dangerous degree. Still, tired and worn to a zombie state, they pressed on, always in silence, their minds weary and spirits dulled. At least another day and a half remained before they reached the river with its cool water and welcomed shade.

By noon their mounts were notably fatigued. Stopping everyone, Labounty ordered them out of the saddle and sponged out the mouths of the horses. He allowed everyone a swallow of water, then they remount and continue.

Bracewell had not yet attempted escape. This Labounty considered thoughtfully. Though he himself had tried to remain awake during the long night, he had at great risk, catnapped in the saddle. It was dangerous, he knew, but what other choice did he have? Rely on the boy? No, he was ready to run, and if not watched closely, would fall easy prey to Bracewell's cunning ways. Could he count on the woman? Maybe? But suppose they were being followed?

A woman from the east as she was, would not through any fault of her own, have any idea what to look or listen for in the darkness of night. Because of that inexperience, it would prove no chore for men on foot to work their way into camp and overtake the lot of them.

Being realistic, Labounty understood full well there was no way he could get through the remainder of the trip without sleep. Already his mind was forgetting little things and sleep was overtaking him more and more frequently, and always without warning. Every muscle in his body ached, feeling heavy and stiff and his eyes were dry as if filled with sand. He was just plain tired. And the longer he went without sleep the better Bracewell liked it.

Every other hour they stopped and rested the horses. The animals were having a rough time of it and were beginning to stumble or stagger from time to time. They needed water to drink, but sponging was all Labounty could afford to give.

Around two they stopped, and everyone found at least a resemblance of shade beneath a small Pinion Tree. Walking out from the others Labounty studied their back trail carefully.

Far off in the distance he thought he saw a small wisp of rising dust, but maybe he had been mistaken; it lasted only a short time and was gone. Perhaps what he saw had only been a dust devil? He was too tired to trust himself, and at this point it was too easy to see things that weren't there.

Satisfied as much as he could be that it was nothing, he walked back to the others and sat in the shade of a tree where he rolled a cigarette. After it was lit, he stretched out on his back and stared up into the afternoon sky.

It was rich with blue and flushed with white billowed clouds. Up there, he thought, existed a totally different world, one tranquil and peaceful. Uncrowded with a backdrop of beautiful open space. He made a face. It was a pity grown men seldom talked of such things; openly sharing the feelings of the soul. All possessed deep thoughts, they just kept them locked away; and in so doing, a good part of their lives was lost because of it. In their heart, all men were curious little boys; yet it seemed all they ever talked about was business and conquests.

"Bet your wishing we were in Yuma, hey friend?"

Instantly Labounty dropped his thoughts and went for his gun. Defensively Bracewell threw up his bound hands.

"Hold it friend, I didn't mean to startle you. I'm just starved for a little man to man conversation if you know what I mean?"

Easing his hand away, Labounty pulled himself into a sitting position keeping his eye on Bracewell. The man sat down opposite him staring at first, not saying anything, but then smiled; a big smile, one false and cunning. He stank of body sweat and dirt and Labounty found him disgusting; of course, he had to admit he himself wasn't much better.

"How long you figure we got till Yuma, friend?" Bracewell asked.

"We'll get there soon enough." Labounty said, desiring no conversation.

Bracewell refused to take the hint. "I heard tell Injuns were mighty thick these parts, war Injuns at that. Reckon we'll meet up with some before we get to where we're going." Bracewell dropped the smile. "If we do, you'll be needing my help".

Taking one last draw on his cigarette, Labounty crushed it beneath his boot heel. Bracewell continued; "Look, I don't know why you're taking a personal interest in this thing, but I'll tell you right now, I'm not planning on going to Yuma, and even if I did, the sheriff couldn't hold me. I have a lot of friends and some of them are not very nice people, if you know what I mean."

Bracewell looked over at the woman. "Young Red there has really caught your fancy, hasn't she?"

He looked back and Labounty gave him a cold stare, but he didn't shut up. "If you're smart," Bracewell continued, "you'll turn me loose now. You and the boy go about your business and leave the woman with me. If you don't, then just maybe none of you will see Yuma." He grinned, "Or is it you've got your own manly sights set on Red." Bracewell glanced again at the woman stretched on her back beneath the Pinion. "She does have a figure worthy of a gun fight. Imagine tearing that dress away and…"

Labounty reached out and grabbed Bracewell by the shirt collar, pulling him close. With clenched teeth he warned him, "you say something like that again and I'll rip you apart. You're a sick animal Bracewell, and your kind are better off behind bars, or dead." Then he shoved him away and rose to his feet. "Mount up," he shouted harshly, "we're riding out!"

Near as he could figure they were within a twenty-four-hour ride to the river. Once there, it would be two more days at most to Yuma.

Mounted, Labounty took the lead pulling Bracewell's horse behind. The hot sun refused to let up, continuing to burn and radiate with relentless cruelty. Despondently the animals pushed on, more mechanical than physical. Climbing an old arroyo embankment Bracewell's mount stumbled and fell, pinning the man's legs and leaving him hanging to one side following its' recovery. Labounty had half a mind to let him hang like that for the remainder of the day but helped him to straighten instead.

Dusk with its cooler temperatures was slow in coming but they had made good time. For that Labounty was thankful. The setting sun had turned the sky brassy and with the heat of day behind, all rode easier in the saddle. Slowly, they were closing the gap.

Early evening was Labounty's favorite time of day. He let his eyes sweep the land through which they rode. Far-reaching in every direction Pinion tree hugged the rock-strewn ground, some tall, but mostly short and twisted. It was an open land of scattered cactus and balls of weightless sage, a place vast and mysterious, void of people and life connected with civilization. Here the population consisted of Gila Monsters, Rattlers and Buzzards, all in constant search for food. It took a great deal of courage for a man to venture here… or stupidity, Labounty thought.

A light breeze cooled his face and he breathed deeply, wondering if he smelled rain in the air. Then he looked down and saw them. They crisscrossed places but were easily noticeably. He guessed eight, maybe nine ponies, all shoeless, and all, if his guess was right, belonged to a war party.

Dismounting, Labounty examined the prints more closely. They were two, maybe three hours old and heading in the direction they were going. Looking up he checked the sky. It was another hour before dark. To ensure distance, he and the others would wait at least thirty minutes before continuing; he possessed no desire to run into the band. So, ordering everyone out of the saddle they took advantage of the wait and rested thankfully.

The break felt good, and all were grateful for the opportunity to stretch their legs. Cub went to a shaded spot and lay down, pulling his big hat over his eyes. The woman sat beneath a tall Pinion and wiped sweat from her brow, then gathered her run of long-hanging hair and pulled it to the top of her head allowing air to reach the back of her neck. Labounty watched her and concluded that at times the long mane, although attractive, must be a bothersome thing.

Bracewell found the shade of a pinion as well, but one that positioned him so he could watch over their back trail.

After resting thirty minutes they remounted and rode on. They traveled for two hours then stopped again, this time making camp. Labounty wanted to ensure they maintained a safe distance between them and the war party. After tying Bracewell to the trunk of a tree Labounty tied the horses a few feet away. The woman cooked a pan of beans and served it with hardtack. Nothing was said during the meal, but everyone ate heartily, famished and weakened from the day's riding.

Total darkness was fast in coming. A partial moon offered little light and Labounty considered it favorable. They had made camp in the middle of a clump of Pinion just off the main trail atop a small knoll.

After he had finished eating, Labounty left the others and positioned himself at the edge of the trees to sit guard. It was a location venting itself out into the open desert and offering a clear view for some distance. Behind him lay the fire and the others, and just beyond them the tied horses. The knoll itself was surrounded by brush on the side facing the opening, and the rest of the area by the trees; little could get through without being heard.

He had been staring into the quiet darkness for some time when Kay walked up behind him. Turning to face her, his eyes caught a glimpse of Cub talking with Bracewell and he yelled sternly.

"Cub, get away from him and turn in. It's late and we have a hard day ahead."

Obviously angered, the boy rose to his feet and stormed quickly to his bedroll where he laid down and jerked the blanket up around him. Tonight, Labounty thought to himself, one of the two, or both, would take a break for it.

Then he remembered the woman and turned to look up at her. She handed him a cup of coffee. "A peace offering," she said, smiling while sitting beside him. "I'd like to try this one more time?"

The night air was quickly cooling as usual and the coffee he knew would hit the spot. She spoke again, her voice gentle in the shadows of the fire.

"I want to apologize for the things I said to you yesterday. I had no right saying them and I'm truly sorry." She stuck out her hand warmly.

"Friends?"

Labounty took it gently into his. It felt as soft as the first time, and somehow smaller, almost fragile. And in his heart, he knew her apology was sincere.

"That's alright, Ms. Martin," he told her. "We're all tired and jumpy."

"Please", she said smiling, "call me Kay".

Labounty nodded. "All right, if you'll call me Jonathan?"

Kay Martin's smile widened and a feeling of warmth she hadn't felt in a long time swept over her. "Yes", she said, "I'd like that".

Without realizing, Labounty continued to hold her hand and they stared. It was awkward but at the same time, stirring. Not sure what to say or do next, they let go, not knowing which one was released first. Kay looked out into the darkness and a silence followed.

The moon hung above their heads in the shape of a perfect rocker and a host of stars filled the sky. Behind them the fire burned softly and filled the area with an easy, gentle light. The desert gave up no sound and they listened to the soft crackling of burning wood.

"Jonathan", Kay said finally, continuing to gaze out into the darkness. "I think I should finish explaining why I'm here."

He glanced at her, "You don't have to, Kay."

"No, I want to", she said turning to look at him back. "I really feel I need to."

Realizing it was important to her, Labounty gave an understanding nod.

"As I had mentioned the other night," she began, "the banker's son would not leave me alone at the party". She paused, choosing her words. "Well, my problems did not end when I left the party that night. Much later, while alone at home, the young man came to call on me again, only this time he forced his way in through a window." She paused again.

Labounty could tell the words were growing harder. Supportively he reached over and squeezed her hand, "Kay, you don't have to go on, it's alright."

"No, please, let me finish." She cleared her throat and Labounty took a sip of coffee.

"There was a struggle." Her voice was strained, and she was just short of tears. "He tried to… take me by force. I tried so hard to stop him, but I was no match. As we struggled, I somehow managed to get to the small dresser near my bed and get this." She pulled a small Derringer from her handbag and held it in her hand. "Anyway, during the struggle I shot him. He died later that night while under the Doctor's care."

Labounty shook his head. "Kay, that was a clear case of self-defense. Surely no court in their right mind would convict you."

"No, not normally. But when your father is wealthy enough to buy and sell half of Chicago, things change. Justice comes cheap."

"Point well taken." Labounty told her.

"Anyway," she went on, "my trial date is set for late next month. A friend from the Chicago police department suggested I get away for a while, out of sight, out of mind as it were. So, I packed up with the intention of heading for San Francisco. I have a sister there." Her face grew sober. "However, I think the boy's father hired guns to track me, and to kill me when they found me."

Suddenly Labounty thought of Bracewell. He whistled under his breath, "You are definitely in a tight spot."

She nodded, "Oh yes. And there's more. While I was in Saint Louis waiting for a train two men began following me. I stayed always with the crowds. When it came time for me to board that night, they were waiting for me by the door."

"Did you recognize these men?"

"No, but I knew very well that they were after me. I fled the station leaving all my belongings behind. They came after me, but I managed to escape into the darkened streets. I walked those streets until the next morning when I bought a horse and saddle, at which time I rode out. From there, after taking a series of coaches and trains, Bracewell and those other two men caught up with me and took me to where you found us. I'm quite sure had it not been for you, my lifeless body would be there now".

Labounty pressed his lips tightly and nodded, reassuring her.

"Well Kay, at least for the time being you're safe and no one is going to hurt you, I promise. When we get to Yuma, I'll go with you, and we'll talk to the Sheriff. He'll help us get it all straightened out. Now why don't you turn in and get some rest?

Kay looked into Labounty's eyes and although she could not see them clearly for the shadows of night, her heart knew they were filled with sincerity.

"Thank you, Jonathan,", she said, "I don't know what I'd do without you. Honestly, you have restored my faith in men and somehow, now, I get the good feeling that maybe things really will work out."

She kissed him softly on the cheek then rose to her feet. She considered kissing him twice but dared not. As she walked to her bedroll Labounty turned and looked out into the dark desert.

What a retreat this was turning out to be, he thought: watching out for a boy who wanted only to run away, not knowing at all what was good for him or the dangers that lay in wait if he did run. One man in bonds, a killer no less, who at any cost would attempt escape, and probably had friends tracking them at this very minute. And finally, Kay, a remarkable woman hunted by hired guns, a lady both tender and kind and innocent… who had kissed him.

Above, the moon shined with partial light and the stars were increasing in number. Behind him the fire had burned down and now offered little relief from the cold. Pulling up his collar he shook his head. Never had any of his excursions turned out so complicated. The way things were going, he wondered if enough time would remain to even allow a return to the mountains.

A cluster of gray clouds buried the moon and a deepened darkness fell over the desert. He wondered about Kay. Did she have a man? If so, was he out there now searching for her? Surely, he was. If Kay were his, he would certainly be.

CHAPTER FOURTEEN

The fire had died some time ago and now red coals glowed undisturbed in the semi-darkness of early morning. A small bird flittered among the Pinion branches but did so in a quiet manner.

Labounty sat quietly with his blanket wrapped close around him. He had sat up through the night on watch, no doubt nodding off and on. Staring out now he studied the open desert, it gave out no sound or movement. The morning dawn was near, just a few minutes away. With it would come the detestable heat… and maybe Indians, or possibly Bracewell's men. He glanced over at the three motionless lumps beneath their blankets.

Bracewell, especially this close to Yuma, was no one to take lightly. He had, so far, weathered the trip with seeming ease, despite his stench. His attempt at breaking loose had to come in the next two days. By noon, or at least mid-day they would be at the river; one more day after that Yuma, then for Bracewell, jail.

Labounty hadn't liked Cub and Bracewell talking; the man was up to something, and he feared it involved the boy. If it did, given Bracewell's past, the youngster would end up hurt or dead. From here on in he would have to remain keenly alert. Truly lives depended on it.

The woman rolled unconsciously onto her back. Of all of them she was having the most difficult time. The hot sun and lack of water was taking its toll, and now that he knew the extent of her problem, he felt a great deal of compassion for her. Hopefully the Sheriff in Yuma could come up with an idea to help her. If not, he had made up his mind to send his own Lawyer to Chicago and investigate the situation. For that matter, he might even go with him.

Cub lay curled in a little ball beneath his blanket. He was really a good boy. Undoubtedly life had dealt him a bad hand, but there was still hope. All he had to do was get him to Yuma, to his family and time would eventually iron it all out.

The fire coals, some still glowing red, and others edged with gray, lay quiet and beckoning, waiting to be fanned back to life. Labounty shivered, pulling the blanket more up around his neck. He yawned tiredly. That was exactly what needed to be done; he'd just have to get up and blow life into the fire. Besides, a hot cup of coffee was what he needed. A cup as big as a washtub, and as hot as…

The hand that touched him startled him and instinctively his right leg kicked out in a wide powerful arc, tripping and throwing the person that had surprised him hard to the ground. He managed to cock the Winchester and aim only seconds before Kay yelled. That yell saved her life.

Clumsily he scrambled to his feet rubbing the hard sleep from his eyes. Kay, now back on her own feet pointed excitedly to the camp. "Jonathan, the boy and Bracewell, they're gone!"

Labounty climbed to his feet and walked to their bedrolls. Each had placed all they could round up beneath the blankets to look as if they were there. Shaking his head, he cursed silently to himself for falling asleep. Then looking to where the horses were tied, he cursed again, they were gone too. Facing Kay, he told her.

"I'm sorry, I didn't mean to knock you down and I certainly did not intend to put you in this situation. Are you alright?"

She nodded. "I'm fine, but you need not apologize. You've gone a long while without sleep to keep us safe. This is certainly not your fault."

"Thanks." He said, appreciative of her support but not in agreement with her.

Realizing there was little they could do now, he began gathering brushes and sticks for a morning fire; when he had it going, Kay put over the cold pot of coffee and he walked about checking on tracks. He rolled a cigarette. Following a long drag he lost himself in thought, thinking aloud. "You dumb, lame-brained kid, how senseless could you be? Running off was bad enough but running off with Bracewell! And before reaching the river."

He made an angry face, mumbling repeatedly, "Dumb kid, dumb kid, dumb kid..."

Kay turned from the fire, "Did you say something, Jonathan?"

"No," he told her, "Not really. Just talking to myself."

"Well, come on and have a cup of coffee. It'll help."

Walking to the fire he tossed his cigarette into the flames and sat. "A cup does sound pretty good right about now", he told her, "but I'm afraid it won't cure what ails me!"

"What do you mean, are we in that much danger?"

Taking the cup from her hands he explained. "No, we'll be okay. It will be difficult, but we'll survive. It's my heart that ails me, it's too big for its own good." Turning he looked soberly off into the distance. "After breakfast, we're going after that fool kid."

She studied him for a moment, noting the serious, long drawn expression. It was a concern that comes from the heart, free of unselfishness and hidden agendas. Turning to gaze into the fire, she sipped her coffee and smiled with an admiration he did not see.

When their cups were empty, they smothered the fire with dirt and gathered their belongings. Bracewell had taken nearly everything; the only exception was Labounty's rifle, handgun, canteen and both his and the Kay's saddle. When they were ready to leave, the woman took up the canteen and he picked up his saddle, throwing it over his shoulder. He left her's behind, not wanting the excess weight.

As they left the shade of the Pinions and stepped out into the now bright sunlight the woman asked, "We have to follow them anyway don't we, since they have the horses?"

Labounty stopped then and pointed with his rifle. "See their tracks going off here in this direction?"

She shaded her eyes with a hand. "Yes."

"Well, they are heading north." Moving the rifle in an eastern direction, he added, pointing with it once again. "They should be going that way, as should we, at least for ten miles or so, that's where the river lays. With the little amount of water, we have left, the horses won't make it another twenty miles, and the next water in the direction they're going is at least fifty. Not a smart move." Labounty shook his head and sighed. "We're going to follow their tracks alright, but not because they have the horses. We must catch up with that fool kid."

The sun was hot on their backs as they walked. Rays reflected off the brown desert floor causing heat waves to shimmer all around. Labounty sighed, so empty and barren was the world in which they trudged.

He would have preferred to wait for the cool of nightfall but there was not time. As it stood, Bracewell and the boy were maybe two hours ahead. Before evening fell, the horses would undoubtedly collapse in exhaustion, leaving the two afoot. Labounty feared it would be at that point Bracewell would leave the youngster behind, moving with haste on foot and not caring that the boy could not keep up. For that reason, it was imperative they did not lose track.

Kay stumbled from time to time, but through effort and determination managed to stay close to his side. He took her hand, pulling her along as they walked, and it helped. The heat burned hot and relentless. Dust filmed their bodies and sweat trickled paths through it.

By noon, they had found shade beside a large brush patch and rested. Labounty told the woman to drink, and she did so eagerly. After three quick sips, she held the canteen out to him. "No," he told her, staring out across the trail they had just covered, "drink some more. Just a swallow will do you no good; in this heat you're just wasting the water. It does nothing for your body, and you may as well have thrown those drops away. Now take three more good, long drinks, then elevate your feet on the saddle."

Without protest, Kay drank, and after handing him the canteen, began to remove her boots. Labounty caught her hand.

"Sorry Kay, leave them on. You take them off now and you won't get them back on your feet. All this walking and heat has caused them to swell."

Too tired to speak, she gave a nod and with effort lifted her tired legs onto the saddle and lay back against the ground. She closed her eyes and within minutes her breathing had become easy and shallow. Propping his own feet Labounty lay beside her and slept himself.

Later, when he awoke, the sun was still up but a light breeze was blowing across the open face of the desert. He checked the sun and guessed they had slept close to an hour, and now evening was but four or less away. He shook Kay lightly. She moved into a sitting position, at first a bit reluctantly. She wanted to sleep longer, and he understood, but it could not be.

"Sorry Kay", he told her, "We've got to move on. There's a light breeze blowing, and it feels good." He watched as she brushed out her hair with her hand and yawned. Smiling, he took out his makings and began rolling a cigarette.

The loud crack of the rifle did not register at first, but when the bullet tore through the loose gathering of his shirtsleeve he dove for the ground, grabbing Kay on his way down. Again, the rifle roared, the bullet tearing into the brush behind them. Crowding themselves behind the saddle Labounty searched the desert quickly and carefully but saw nothing. Training his eyes on the far horizon he searched again, sweeping slowly and gradually inward, working over the terrain, holding on any object where a man might hide behind.

Again, the invisible rifle roared. This time the bullet ripped into the out-stretched stirrup of the saddle. It kicked up wildly then fell still. Only one rifle was being fired, so more than likely there was only one man, maybe two, with the second working around to the back or side in hopes for a clear shot at them.

Sweat trickled down Labounty's face, tracing its way through the film of dust. Despondently he stared into the dancing heat waves. The shooter was out there somewhere, but where? And who was it? Bracewell? Indians? Or some stray desperado who by chance happened to stumble upon their misfortune? That would be just his luck.

Another bullet kicked up dirt to their right. Labounty gripped his rifle with frustration. His eyes watched and stared, hoping for even the slightest movement, but the quiet desert refused to give up the shooter's concealment.

Carefully he searched for anything even remotely out of place. Scattered mesquite brush wavered gently against the wind and the yellow flower of the Prickly Pear Cactus lay open and beckoning to the sun. Pinion tree branches swayed slightly beneath the breeze gathering slow momentum, and beyond all this the shimmering heat waves fluttered above the floor. But he could see no man.

Again, the rifle barked, its report echoing loudly across the desert, this time the bullet creasing the tip of the saddle pommel and barely missing Kay's head.

Frustrated, Labounty laid quietly, giving thought to the situation. The bullets had all hit extremely close. The first through his sleeve, the second in the brush above their heads, the third shattered the stirrup, and the fourth, the saddle's pommel. The shots had all been accurate, and because of this he guessed the rifleman to be no more than a few hundred feet away.

Keeping his head low, he examined the pommel of the saddle. The crease left by the bullet indicated that it came from straight on with the shooter lying close to the ground. He began another search.

The wind was steadily increasing and gently rattled the brush behind them. The sun was cooling and evening was well on its way. Far off to their left came a faint rumbling. Labounty stopped his roving eyes suddenly. Behind a small patch of mesquite brush the ground looked to be a shade lighter than the area around it. He trained his eyes there and did not move them. After a short time, he picked up the slight glitter of an object against the sun, but he blinked, and it was gone.

He played a hunch; resting his rifle across the saddle he took aim on the heart of the brush patch and gingerly took up the slack on the trigger. Halfway home, he pulled, and the big Winchester kicked up wildly with the sound racing off across the desert. Without hesitation he levered the rifle twice more shooting both to the left and right of the brush area.

When his last shot fell quiet, silence smothered the desert and he waited. He thought the light shaded spot he had seen was gone, but he couldn't be sure; at least now nothing glittered.

The wind picked up with sudden vigor rustling its way through the brush. It moaned and coupled with its coolness he tasted moisture in the air. Rain, Labounty guessed, would be falling before the dark of night. Patiently he waited, watching with total alertness. Uncertain, he lay behind the saddle, watchful and with the perseverance of an Apache.

Then it happened! A man rose suddenly from behind the distant brush and ran for all he was worth to Labounty's right. Three times Labounty levered and triggered his rifle, each time kicking up dirt at the man's heels. He berated himself angrily at the misses and rose swiftly to his feet in pursuit. As he left the security of the saddle, he yelled for Kay to remain.

Although hesitant, she did as told, watching him go until his running form faded into the desert. Alone she waited, growing impatient, worried, straining her ears and eyes, wishing she could see beyond the desert obstacles. Minutes passed with the only sound being that of the increasing wind.

Then a shot sounded, two shots, now three, each distant and frightening, then silence. The wind blew a few wisps of hair across her face, and she brushed them away with her hand. Her muscles ached and her skin burned where the sun had been making it red.

There alone, she thought about Chicago, of its cold and frosty winters, its nightlife and its people, its glitter and glamour. She thought about her hotel and wondered how it was doing. Then she thought about Labounty. Was he still alive? She prayed he was. And not just because he was protecting her, more so because he was different, special, a cut above any other man she had ever met.

He was a gentleman… a true gentleman, a man free of airs and honestly thoughtful in an innocent unconscious way. And he had risked his life for a woman he knew nothing about, and now escorted the same through a land filled with tortures and easy death. He was out there now, for her, and for a small boy too young to appreciate the kind and compassionate ways of this quiet, gentle man.

The big hand slipped suddenly around her mouth so forcefully she felt pain shoot through her entire face. A strong, muscular body lifted her with ease and secured her arms at the same time. Her head lay pressed against a huge chest, and she could not move. Wildly her heart pounded with fear and in her mind she wondered about three things… Jonathan Labounty, the little boy he cared so much about, and if she would be alive come sunrise.

CHAPTER FIFTEEN

Labounty awoke with his head afire; a burning pain that stung like smoldering flesh. The sun was hot on his back and drying blood had mixed with the tiny stones and dirt beneath him, forming a crude natural bandage. His eyes were blurred, his head swam with dizziness, and nowhere could he find the strength to rise.

Quiet, he lay motionless trying to recall what had happened, wondering why the ground beneath his head felt crusty. The wind blew with strong force, kicking up dirt and tossing tumbleweed. It felt cool on his skin and blew teasingly at his hair. Then, somehow, he managed to rise to his knees, his heart pounding in his head. Lifting a hand, he touched the crusted spot on his forehead and made a face as waves of pain shot through him. His mind, like his body, felt numb and unworkable, a distant thing, far out of reach. He could not motivate himself or reason, only cry out at the pain trying so hard to make him yield, to lie down and surrender, to give up and give in to the soft beckoning fingers of death.

Then he remembered the running man, the dodging of cactus and brush, and the sound of a rifle… no, three rifles. Or was it one rifle fired repeatedly? Taking a deep breath, he fought the urge to faint; how many rifles really didn't matter now. What he really wondered most was whose rifle it was; for the shots hadn't come from the man he'd been chasing.

The pain did not ease and showed no sign of doing so. He thought of the sun: it was still up and hot, just as hot now as it was when that bullet had torn the flesh from his head. So maybe he hadn't been unconscious for a long time.

The wind blew with a strange, definitive power, whipping at his hair and clothing. A huge ball of tumbleweed brushed his leg then blew into a small pinion tree and hung up. Labounty's body trembled in need of strength, and his head screamed against the pain. He wanted very much to lie down and close his eyes. His body coaxed him, begged him to do so; to forget what was past and to accept the pleasurable relief the closing of his eyes would bring. But he remained, and without looking up, shouted into the desert, "NO."

The pain was damnable, and the persistent wind howled and blew, gaining in strength, creating wild swirls of sand. Tumbleweed crashed endlessly into the desert growth, and he knew he must get up and move. Grabbing the rifle lying at his side, he propped himself on it and stood. The ground spun, and the white and blue colors of the sky clashed as he dropped to his knees, grimacing.

Waiting a few minutes, he stood again, this time remaining a long while, weaving as he stood. Then he voluntarily lowered himself to the ground. The pain was slowly diminishing, and he knew he was winning. Several times he rose and lowered himself, until finally, the pain was little more than a throbbing headache, and he was able to walk.

Stopping to rest several times along the way, he made his way back to the saddle and lowered himself down into the shade. The saddle and area around it were as he had left it, except for Kay, she was gone. Angrily, he clenched his teeth and swore.

Above, the sky was blue with a few scattered fluff-white clouds. Off in the distance to the west, it rumbled faintly and showed the color of black slate.

While resting, Labounty examined the tracks around him. One man had been there, and judging from the torn-up ground, had struggled with Kay. The tracks belonging to the man were cut long and deep - the print of a large fellow, very possibly Bracewell. And if so, Labounty wondered, where was Cub?

Also near the saddle lay the makings he had dropped when the first bullet struck. Reaching, he picked them up and built a cigarette. The pain in his head was easing rapidly, so after the smoke he would begin following the tracks. The rain, when it hit, would be a welcome thing, for the canteen he had left by the saddle was gone, and he was yet a good many miles from the river.

Total, he sat less than five minutes before crushing out the cigarette. Slowly he rose. Picking up his saddle, he swung it over his shoulder and made a face as his heart pounded in his head. The tracks moved off to the west in the direction of the river… and toward the approaching storm. They also indicated that the woman was still struggling; that thought delighted Labounty. He grinned and told Kay to give him hell.

Half a mile on the trail, he found a spot where the two had come upon five riders, or at least it appeared to be five riders. The tracks of two of the horses were not cut as deep as the others, and they could have been empty saddled. The ground here gave no indication there had been a struggle other than Kay, so Labounty guessed they were men known to her captor. All five animals were shod.

Anger filled Labounty's veins, and concern for the woman filled his heart. He stood there amid the howling wind and blowing sand, seeking a decision. To follow East was to go after Kay, and who knew what sort of men held her. What they would do to her. If they were those hired in Chicago, then they would do one of two things: return her there or kill her here in their own time and in their own way. And if one of them was in fact Bracewell, then there was no doubt, she would never see home again. Labounty sighed long and hard. On the other hand, he could turn and continue north where he had last seen Cub's tracks.

While sorting his thoughts Labounty looked up into the sky. It had grown much darker in only a few minutes. By now, he reasoned, the horses

Bracewell and the boy had been riding were down, and the two would be on foot; that is if Kay's captor was not Bracewell. The way he saw it, there were a couple of ways he could look at it: first, Bracewell went north with a definite purpose in mind, like maybe meeting someone he knew. Five horses had met Kay and her captive at this point, and there had been no sign of a struggle among them. Were the two held at gunpoint, or did the man with her know the riders?

Too many questions remained unanswered: like why was he left alive? Had they run out of time and been unable to risk making sure of his death, or were they just confident of their shots? Who did the five horses belong to, and where was the boy? Regardless of which way he chose to go, the rain would hit long before he reached the end of either trail.

This was open country and once the rain started, it would become almost impossible to follow any tracks, and the possible directions or reasons for travel were just too vast. Labounty shrugged, within minutes the rain would begin washing away all signs. The riders were headed for the river, and in all probability, would not stop until they reached it, making camp the moment they did. If he stuck to their trail as long as possible, and continued on until he reached the river himself, then perhaps he could find their camp before sunup. And if he did… maybe, just maybe, make a double rescue; an innocent woman and if lucky, a small lost little boy. Based of course, on not getting himself killed.

As for Cub, he was a sly one, a stinker yes, but also a thinker; and now knew how to find his way to the river. And if he was separated from Bracewell, then it was there he would head, and probably reach it by noon tomorrow, or there abouts.

A sudden gust of wind nearly blew the hat from Labounty's head, and he caught it barely in time. To his right and left, the sky rumbled, and lightning flashed. The wind was growing wild. He tied his bandana around his mouth and nose and made his decision. Turning East, he moved off following the easy tracks of five riders… but heavy in his heart and fresh on his mind lingered the sight of a small boy in a large hat and raggedy old coat with the sleeves rolled up. Without realizing, Labounty showed a faint smile. "The boy would make it," he told himself, the boy will make it."

CHAPTER SIXTEEN

Night came quickly. And when he could no longer see the tracks, Labounty dropped his saddle and sat beside it. Pushing on through the wind and darkness and an impending storm was an option, but the odds of finding the river or even traveling in the right direction for that matter, would be nearly impossible. The dark sky held no stars and was hiding the moon, and without them by which to navigate, the chance of traveling in circles was far too great.

So, conceding to the elements, he pulled himself to his knees, turned his back to the wind and in the cold blackness untied his blanket. Laying down beside the saddle he wrapped himself tightly within it and waited.

The wind pushed hard, hurling mesquite brush into the Pinion and flinging gritted sand; it howled angrily at the cold night and blew fiercely at the blanket covering him. Cold and tired he lay there, encased within his wool cocoon; a lone man who held the only hope for a small boy and a beautiful woman. And yet in the big scheme of things, he was little more than like a drop of rain in the center of a great tempestuous expanse. Holding the blanket tight around him he fought to keep the swirling sand free of his face. Twice he choked and had a difficult time catching his breath. Minutes passed in segments of time unable to track, then the rain began. At first it was a light, barely noticeable scattering of wet drops. But within minutes its tempo increased, and it fell like a mad cold hammering; quickly soaking both his blanket and him.

Over the desert it grew bitterly cold. He lay there alone, wet to the skin and shivering, and in the solitude of his thoughts time crept slowly past. The wind was cruel, pushing and pulling at his blanket, with his teeth chattering beneath the soggy covering; thoughts and memories leaped endlessly through his mind; good things and bad things and things he thought he had long forgotten. But lost in those thoughts along with repeated short fragments of sleep, there finally came the moment he laid so long hoping for; the storm had passed.

Throwing off the sodden blanket, he stood. There was a hand full of stars now, and above his head a three-quarter moon was pouring down its slivery-gray light. Around him the ground lay spotted with puddles of water. Stepping out of the very one he had been forced to lay in, he studied the stars and calculated his desired direction. When done, he picked up his belongings, and following a small prayer to the Maker, he started for the river.

CHAPTER SEVENTEEN

He found them camped along the bank as he had hoped. Their fire glowed brightly in the gray dawn of early morning, and around the fire all slept but one. With a walk of boredom, a guard carrying a Winchester paced the clearing in which they were camped. Several times he stopped at the high bank near the river's edge and kicked tiny stones into the swift, running water.

About the fire, four motionless figures slumbered peacefully. One of those sleeping figures was Kay. Fifty feet behind them were four horses cropping noisily on wet grass.

Labounty lay in high brush along the riverbank. What he should do, he thought, was advance the camp and gun down anyone who made a move. But cold-blooded killing was not in him. If he could take out the guard maybe he could get into the camp and hold the others at gunpoint, then he and Kay could ride out.

The sky was growing lighter, and he knew the sun would be coming up anytime. When it did those that slept would begin to rise. If he was going to do something it had to be fast.

Quietly, he watched the guard, studying his movements and pattern. Mostly he lingered near the fire, straying only to walk to the water's edge. So, it was there Labounty thought, he would give the man a surprise.

Crawling carefully through the wet brush he lowered himself over the bank to the water. Then, taking great pain while fighting the current, worked his way across until he was just this side of where the guard made his stops at the bank above. Quietly he gathered three small stones from the muddy bank and held them in his right hand; the left gripped his rifle. Then he waited.

Far off to the east a small tip of sun peaked over the horizon. Morning would soon burst into a radiant light, and he knew time was working against him. If the guard failed to make one more trip to the bank then he would have no choice but to kill him and charge those sleeping.

Along the bank itself the ground was thick with soft reddish mud, the result of the hard driving rain. Much of the tall grass running along the river's edge had been flattened by the wind and now lay pressed against the ground. The sun rose higher, now climbing steadily above the horizon. Golden light was spreading rapidly across the sleeping desert and for Labounty time had run out.

Then, something plopped into the water just ahead of him. Carefully, he glanced up and saw the guard standing there staring out across the open land at the distant Sun rise. His back was too him.

With caution and careful aim, Labounty tossed one of the stones he had picked up into the water just beyond where the guard stood. When it splashed, the man immediately turned toward the noise and crouched low. Labounty tossed another and heard the cock of the Winchester.

The sun was nearly above the horizon. He tossed the third and when it plunked into the water the guard lowered himself down over the bank. That was when Labounty put his rifle barrel to the man's neck.

"Mister," he told him in a whisper, taking his rifle from his hand and laying it up on the bank, "you left me back there with what you thought was a bullet in my head, believing I was dead. You miscalculated. I ought to kill you now because of it, but I won't. Remember this, when I leave here, just keep moving and forget you ever laid eyes on me. If you don't, then the next time we meet I'll introduce you to the other end of my rifle."

With great force, Labounty swung the butt of his Winchester catching the man behind the head. Grabbing his limp body before it tumbled into the water, he laid him quietly at the muddy shoreline then scurried up over the bank. When he was near the fire, he leveled his rifle and fired off a shot. The loud report raced off across the open plains and at the same time, three of the four sleeping figures grabbed for their guns.

"I wouldn't do that." Labounty's voice was loud, calm, sure, and very much a surprise. The men froze where they were, slowly easing back their hands.

"Get up the lot of you," he said coldly, "keep your hands high over your heads and file away from the saddles and blankets."

Kay rose to her feet with a smile as big as the giant ball of sun that was rising above their heads. Daylight was spreading everywhere, and she loved the beginning of this new day.

Bracewell was angry but tried to hide it. Looking at Labounty he smiled. "Well friend, you're a hard case to do in. I figured we had made a mistake not checking on you. But what can a man say except live and learn?" Bracewell held out his hands in a mocking gesture. "So, go ahead friend," he said holding his smile. "Shoot us down and leave us for the buzzards." The others looked at him as though he were crazy.

Now Labounty smiled.

"I have to give you credit, Bracewell. For a man as stupid as you, you certainly know your psychology. But don't flatter yourself. The reason I'm not going to gun you down has nothing to do with you conning me. It's because murdering isn't the way I do things. But I will tell you this; when the woman and I leave here you had better forget we exist. Because the next time I see you, I will kill you, and that's a promise. And that goes for all of you". Labounty glanced at the others to ensure they heard clearly. "Now, one question and we'll be on our way. Where is the boy?"

Bracewell grinned mockingly, feeling he now had the upper hand. "Go to hell."

Taking three steps Labounty moved close and directly in front of Bracewell. "You know", he said, "you're as likable as the smell and taste of rotting Buffalo meat served at a Sunday Social on a hot afternoon".

Bracewell frowned, pondering the words. Labounty smiled. This is for Cub. He swung his rifle in a powerful arch, catching Bracewell under the chin. A loud crack broke the stillness of the morning and the force of the blow lifted Bracewell's free of the ground and slamming hard into the wet grass unconscious.

Quickly moving his eyes to the others and holding his stare, he told Kay. "Get one of the blankets and spread it on the ground. I want every gun, knife and boot piled into it. When it's done, tie it off."

At first, the standing men began to protest and make angry faces, but Labounty smiled and reassured them. "Fellows, it's near fifty miles to Yuma and the walk will do you good. Besides, a little stroll in the sunshine beats a bullet in the head if you know what I mean?" He then had the men saddle the pack-mule and two of the horses. When Kay had the blanket filled, Labounty had one of them tie it to the mule as well, then he and Kay mounted up. Pulling a spare horse behind, they chased the extras away as they rode out. Reining south they rode downstream toward Yuma.

With Bracewell still unconscious the standing men stood in the clearing behind shaking their fists and yelling into the now bright light of an already searing sun. Labounty shook his head, their language was worse than Cub's.

As soon as they were out of sight, Labounty found a safe place to cross the river and turned back east, riding out into the open ground leaving the river to their backs. For nearly six miles they rode in that direction before stopping to make a quick breakfast.

He built a small fire and Kay put over a pot of coffee. Waiting for it to boil she took the opportunity to clean and dress his scalp wound. She warmed water and when it was hot, Labounty went to the pack-mule where he retrieved his container of ointment along with one of his only two clean shirts. After ripping it in strips, she washed the cut, applied the ointment and then bandaged it. She also cleaned and redressed his neck.

Once breakfast was over they broke camp and climbed back into the saddles. This time Labounty turned north.

The woman looked over at him admiringly.

"You're going after the boy, aren't you?"

Not looking at her, he gave a nod offering no conversation.

"You really like him, don't you Jonathan"? She studied his face while continuing to talk. "He is an adorable little guy, and extremely mature and responsible for his age I think," a wisp of a smile showed at the corners of her mouth, "and certainly a young man with a mind of his own".

Looking away then, Kay shaded her eyes with her hand to look off into the distance. She stared out over the openness but was not looking at anything. When she turned back, she asked. "Jonathan, do you think Bracewell might have hurt him?"

This time Labounty looked at her. "He's alive Kay. I know he is."

By noon they were back at the spot where he had left Kay's saddle. That's where they found him. He lay face down, just off the trail beneath a small Pinion. In haste they left their horses and rushed to his side. Labounty felt his heart pound as he rolled the boy over. When he did, Cub looked up and when he saw who it was, he smiled. "Hot damn, about time Jonathan Labounty. Got a shot of water for a thirsty man?"

Closing his eyes, Labounty hugged him.

Together, the three rested there. For lunch, they ate hardtack and drank warm water. Cub sat near Labounty and as he ate, he told him. "I'm sorry for runnin' away like I did. I know I should a listened, but Bracewell filled my brain with horseshit." Embarrassed suddenly, Cub looked at Kay, "Bull crap I mean." Kay hid her smile. Then Cub looked back to Labounty. "The liar told me so much I didn't know what to believe. Said he knew folks in California that would be glad to put me to work, that he'd take me there himself if I turned him loose. And he said you were all wrong for trying to put me in a family, that I was a man and should be treated a whole lot better than the way you were treatin' me."

Labounty shrugged. "And what do you think about it all that now, Cub?"

The boy looked him squarely in the eyes, "I gotta' be honest with ya Jonathan Labounty. What I done was dumber than a big-petered man in a New Orleans whore house eaten' saltpeter for lunch."

Labounty made a terrible face, embarrassed for Kay. Labounty glanced quickly at Kay then back to Cub, and demanded, "and what in the...heck, do you know about saltpeter?"

Cub shrugged, "Hell..., heck, I don't know. Red talked about needin' to eat come fer he went into the..." Cub went silent and again glanced at Kay, then back at Labounty, and lowering his voice told him, "You know, that girl place. Where men do grown up stuff to the ladies!"

"Boy," Labounty said shaking his head, "what's the matter with you? You don't even know what you just said even means."

He flushed. "No, not exactly I reckon. I just heard Red and the others talk about it."

"Cub, honestly, I just don't know what to do with that mouth of yours."

Cub cut in. " I can't help myself, it's just the way I talk, like Old Red and them."

"Old Red and them or not," Labounty said, "next time you say something like that, even if you don't know what it means, I'm washing your mouth out with soap. And there won't be any bet going on this time. You understand me?"

Looking down at his feet Cub replied almost in a whisper, "Yes sir."

Kay rose and walked to the pack-mule, hiding her smile again.

Labounty took a drink of water from his canteen. He was angry at Cub, but then again, he had been young once himself. The boy was growing up. The trouble was, he had had the wrong kind of teachers for the last few years.

Placing the cork back into his canteen he turned and studied the boy who was still staring down at his feet. There was hope for him, of that he was confident, all he had to do was get him to Yuma, to his family, and once there, convince him he needed to stay.

Then Cub looked up and caught his eye.

"I'm sorry Mr. Labounty," he said apologetically, "I promise I'll try and not talk like that no more." Looking toward Kay standing by the mule he told her in a loud voice, "and, ma'am, I really am sorry." Kay threw him a wink. Cub rose to his feet then and said something that took Labounty by surprise.

"Well, I ain't sayin' it but one time only. I reckon it's time we start ridin' for Yuma?"

Stunned and speechless, Labounty stared at him. A few seconds passed, and a faint smile appeared. He looked at Kay and she matched the smile.

CHAPTER EIGHTEEN

The circling Buzzards indicated something, or someone was dead or dying in the desert heat. So, with caution the three rode to that location.

The brown muscular body glistened beneath the bright sunlight and lay face down upon the hard ground. Labounty studied both the motionless form and area around it with caution. At first, he thought the man dead, but just to be safe assumed the opposite, suspecting him a possible kingpin of some trick.

It was obvious they had come upon an Indian, an Apache. Though an older man, perhaps early sixties, he was well built with broad shoulders and thick back muscles. His face lay on the left side and turned toward them. The Indian possessed the facial structure of a typical Apache, flat faced with wide nose and distinctive cheekbones. He wore only a loincloth with moccasins and deer-hide leggings. Near his right shoulder lay a decorative headband. His long, silver-black hair glistened beneath the bright rays of the sun. At his left side lay a broken bow and crushed quiver of arrows.

As they drew closer Labounty pulled his rifle from its scabbard and laid it across his saddle in front of him. Cautiously they continued.

The ground about the body had been torn up by horses; shod horses, not shoeless Indian Ponies. So far, he had seen no visible wounds on the body.

Above their heads the horde of buzzards continued to circle, drawing closer and impatient. The scorching desert remained a quiet, noiseless terrain. Then Labounty saw the blood. A small puddle had soaked into the ground leaving a dark stain atop the sun-baked dirt. Satisfied it was no trick he left his horse quickly and went to the Indian.

Kneeling, he checked what he could, then rolled the body over. The injury was obvious. On the lower left side of the abdomen, he found a gunshot wound. It had crusted over and now looked inflamed and reddened with infection. The man had been lying there for some time, but he was still alive.

Working together the three moved the body into the shade of two intermingled Pinion trees then turned to doing the necessary things to help the dying man. At this point his breathing was shallow and pulse weak.

Cub gathered wood for a fire and the woman prepared a pan of water for boiling. Labounty went to the pack-mule and rummaged through the canvas bags.

The Indian, as near as he could guess, had been shot sometime within the past couple of days. The bullet had entered the abdomen but had not exited. It was now lodged somewhere inside the body, and this deeply concerned him since bullet wounds were totally unpredictable. Sometimes a slug entering one area traveled a good distance to another before stopping, leaving no clue where it ended up; and all the while it tumbled through the body it tore up tissue and ripped through body organs, leaving behind internal bleeding most often fatal.

If the Indian was lucky this bullet was near where it had entered. For if it was not, then too much probing for it could cost the man his life. This was Labounty's dilemma; the probing in itself could kill him, yet without an attempt at finding it there would be no hope at all.

Pulling open the last of the canvas bags he found what he was looking for, a full bottle of whiskey, one hundred-proof. If anything was going to help the dying Indian, this would. Finally, he grabbed the last clean shirt then returned to the others. By the time he was back with them Cub had the fire going and the water was nearly boiling.

After placing the Indian on a blanket Labounty laid the blade of his knife into the open flames then sat back and waited.

The air around them was sticky and humid, a lingering annoyance that made breathing difficult, creating that much more danger to the unconscious Indian. Overhead the buzzards continued to circle, waiting for what they considered rightfully theirs.

Labounty rolled a cigarette. After lighting it he inhaled deeply and gave thought to the situation. It was, he felt, disastrous at best. If the smoke from the fire did not attract Bracewell and his men, then the buzzards circling above would. And even if Bracewell didn't show up, an Indian war party might.

He looked thoughtfully at the unconscious man. Could he himself be part of a war party? If so, and Indians came, would they just attack thinking they were the ones that had done this to their comrade, or would they want to parlay, asking for explanations first? And even if they did, would they believe it anyway?

Their position near the Pinions amounted to nothing strategically. There was no defense, no cover and no place to go. The horses were exposed, and they themselves were exposed. Yet, what else could they do? Leave the Indian? No, he was dying, and although slim, ran a chance of pulling through if attended to immediately and not moved.

Labounty drew heavily on his cigarette; he was putting all their lives at risk for a stranger, a potential hostile even. But dislike it as he may, that was not the issue. What really mattered was that a human life was at stake and an attempt at saving it must be made, even if it did mean risking their own.

Crushing out his cigarette Labounty rinsed his hands using some of the hot water from the pan. After withdrawing the knife from the fire, he watched a light curl of smoke rise from the hot blade. Then, with a steady hand, he poured a light film of whiskey over the infected area.

He was not a surgeon and made no pretense of being such. But during the war he had seen more than his share of it, and had on several occasions assisted the physicians following intense fighting. The Indian's life would depend upon what he remembered… and a lot of luck.

As soon as he had made the initial incision, the wound began seeping. The woman had cut the shirt into pieces and now used the same to sop up the liquid running out from the wound site. It smelled of infection, and Kay made a face. Slowly, Labounty cut deeper into the Indian's flesh, searching for the bullet. Sweat mounted on his forehead and ran down his face. Several times he had Cub wipe his brow. Feverishly his fingers probed the open cut, searching frantically.

Continuously, blood and infected body fluid seeped from the wound. Cub watched with interest. The buzzards remained in the sky defying the efforts of the three humans trying so hard to deny them their feast.

Labounty worked with jaw tightly clenched, remaining focused, yet occasionally looking up and searching the distance.

"Anything yet?" Kay asked hopefully.

He shook his head with despair. Off in the distance, something caught his eye. A movement, and it was only by chance he had glimpsed it. Squinting, he looked for it again but nothing moved.

His fingers continued to probe and the sweat that ran down into his eyes irritated him. Then, he found it. Looking up into the Kay's eyes he smiled.

"Got it."

With slow, careful fingers he worked the little ball of lead to the surface and when it was finally out leaned back and sighed while wiping his sleeve across his forehead. Then he told Cub.

"Go to the packsaddle, left side forward compartment and bring me the sewing kit there". Cub rose to his feet and darted for the gear. As an afterthought Labounty shouted, "also, bring me the tin of ointment." Nodding, the boy turned and hurried to get the things Jonathan Labounty had asked for.

When he returned, he watched in astonishment as Labounty poured whiskey into the wound site then sewed up the opening using needle and thread. He then had the woman wash the area with hot water. As soon as she was finished, he poured whiskey over the site one more time. Then, after applying a coating of ointment dressed and bandaged the area.

There remained nothing else to do now but wait. The Indian's chances were at best fifty-fifty. By night, a strong fever would come, and it would be up to the Indian's own willpower as to whether he fought for life or gave up.

The boy sat patiently at the Indian's side while Kay poured Labounty a cup of coffee. He took it thankfully. Following a sip, he stood and put the fire out. At first Kay protested, wanting to keep the coffee hot and pointing out that the buzzards flying overhead would give away their position anyway, so the smoke made by the fire mattered very little regarding someone spotting them. Labounty smiled, impressed that an eastern woman would think so logically.

Sitting back down beside her he explained.

"Kay, you're probably right about the fire and Buzzards. However, if someone were to spot the Birds overhead, they may just think it's an animal and not ride to see. But when you see a column of smoke from a cooking fire then it leaves no doubt". Labounty wiped a run of sweat from him forehead. "But actually, there's another reason for putting the fire out now. Should Bracewell or a War Party happen to be nearby, then it could give us an edge later". Her green eyes widened questioningly and Labounty marveled at their brightness.

"What do you mean?"

"Well, the Indian needs rest, at least a few hours before we move him. If we leave the fire out beginning now and wait several hours before riding out, then whoever finds our campsite and finds the fire ash cold, they will believe we are long ahead of them, when actually we may only be a very short distance. If things get tight that could give us an edge. The element of surprise is always a plus.

"Oh, I see," she said smiling. "You know Jonathan Labounty, you're quite a talented and interesting man."

Pleased but embarrassed, he looked away, out into the quiet desert.

The open land lay still and silent, except for the circling buzzards. But back in the dark recesses of his mind he wondered what that movement had been earlier.

After finishing his coffee, he rose to his feet and withdrew his knife from its sheath. Kay watched him disappear into the desert north of camp. She was curious as to what he was up to but did not ask.

Within the hour he returned with poles from scattered Pinion trees and constructed a crude but effective travois on which to pull the Indian. He then attached it to the mule. Cub, who had never left the Indian's side, was dozing, as was Kay. He let them rest another hour then woke them.

They packed up camp then gently loaded the Indian onto the travois. The air remained hot, but the sun had begun to set. In a short time, night would fall and things would cool down. Labounty disliked the idea of moving the Indian but there was no other choice. They had to find a more secure location to hold up. A place where they could sit and wait until the Indian's fever broke and he was able to ride. With luck they would find such a place before dark, and with a little more luck, the Indian would not die before they found it.

CHAPTER NINETEEN

They made a new camp along the river in the concealment of heavy brush. The Pinion had thinned and like the trees, the cacti had grown sparse as well. So, the desert on either side of the river stretched outward little more than an empty stretch of hell.

Leaving the Indian in Kay's care Labounty rode out and tried covering their tracks for at least a mile back. The travois had cut furrows into the earth and its path was almost impossible to hide.

He knew there was no way of totally shaking Bracewell and his men, only temporarily avoiding them. Sooner or later there would come a kill or be-killed showdown, and this time there would be no hesitation to using his gun. Right now, however, that confrontation for as long as possible, needed to be avoided for the Indian's sake.

The sun was but a fragment of yellow wrapped in crimson when he returned to camp. Night was here. There had been no change in the Indian, so he rolled a cigarette and sat down near the edge of the brush patch. Tiredly, Kay came over and sat beside him wrapping her arms around her knees. Glancing at the Indian then looking at Labounty she asked. "Do you think he'll make it?" The infection does seem to be staying where it's at."

Labounty shook his head looking at the unconscious Indian.

"I don't know, Kay. I'd have to say his chances are fair." He pulled his eyes back to her. "The area where we found him had been torn up by several men on horseback. My guess is those men gave him a rough time before they shot him. You can bet he has a heart full of bad feelings. And sometimes hate can fuel determination."

The woman nodded, "Yeah, I can understand how he might feel."

Labounty nodded silently and looked away.

The last of the sun dropped out of sight taking with it the final remains of warmth. Turning, he told Cub to put an extra blanket over the Indian. The boy did as he was told and Labounty watched him.

He had not allowed a fire for fear of it drawing attention. Bracewell and his men were probably still on foot and many miles behind, but because of the tracks found around the Indian he couldn't be sure. The men who had shot the Apache may have been more of Bracewell's crew and had already found the bootless killer and his cohorts. And now the whole lot of them may once again be hunting for Kay.

Stars were beginning to show, and the dark face of the Colorado River reflected the bright light of the full moon. There was a calm across the open land, a peacefulness that felt good. A single coyote howled at the moonlight somewhere far away and even that seemed becoming of the quiet night. As darkness came and rest supplied their needs, peace remained around them.

The early morning sky was still filled with stars when the shadowy form closed the farmhouse door behind him, careful not to wake his wife.

Looking up into the twinkling luster he admired their God crafted beauty then stepped off the porch and walked whistling to the barn.

He was a proud and happy man. Though many in town teased and made fun tagging him the local sodbuster, he took it in stride. For he loved what he did and was proud of the fields he furrowed and the bountiful crops they produced. Proud too was he of his wife, Bonnie. Though married only a short time, and new to the ways of farming, she had held up surprisingly well in this strange hard land. Because she had come from well-to-do Boston blood, he had had his doubts when they moved west. But now there were none and pride filled his veins. Thinking of her he smiled wider.

Now at the barn door he paused, wondering about an unfamiliar noise that had caught his ear. Because it lasted only a second, he shrugged it away and entered into the building's dark interior. Loose hay crunched beneath his feet as he groped his way to the center pole where the barn lantern hung. His left hand found the beam, then the big spike upon which it hung; but the lantern was missing.

Odd, he thought, he was sure he had placed it there before going up to the house last night. Then suddenly a surge of panic flushed over him and somehow, he knew his time had come. He called out to Bonnie, perhaps to warn her, or maybe to say her name just one more time.

The hand went over his mouth only seconds before the hay-hook ripped into his chest. Twice he felt the sharp sting of the curved hook but only the first time did it cause him great pain. The second thrust was little more than a distant sound that faded away with his last breath.

Through the darkness of morning the four silent figures crept their way toward the small farmhouse. An oil lantern, turned low, sat in the middle of the kitchen table and at the black iron stove a young unsuspecting woman fed wood pieces into the high-dancing, yellow flames. She hummed as she worked.

Then the door swung open suddenly, crashing against the inner wall. A hinge broke and it hung at an awkward angle. The woman's scream caught in her throat as she whirled around, her hand covering her mouth in shock.

The four men that poured through the door were dirty and unshaven. And odd to her none were wearing boots.

The biggest of the four, leaving the others behind in a group, crossed the floor to where she stood. He was grinning. Towering high above her he pressed his body against hers, pinning her forcefully against the stove. Held in terror she could not move, her heart pounded, and tears welled in her eyes. With a dirty hand he stroked her hair.

She stood quivering beneath his filthy touch, wondering what had become of the man she loved. But in her heart she knew what his fate had been based on the four reprobates now standing in her house; and without wanting to visualize it, she knew too what hers was to be. The big man pressing hard against her grabbed a fist of hair and pulled her head back brutally.

"Honey," he told her, voice lewd with decadence and foul breath, "you got some right pretty hair. So soft and shiny, the kind a man likes to get his fingers in." He gave it a light tug again and she bit down on her lip to help defer the need to scream. Tears were running down her cheeks now and she wanted to run, but there was no getting free of him, he was far too strong, and even if she were able, there was no place to go; and no one to go to for help.

Her husband lay dead somewhere outside the door and she knew they would eventually rape her then kill her too. These men were spawns of the devil and fate was clearly leaning on the side of evil.

"You know what I like more than real pretty hair, honey?" The big man said tightening his grip and stroking her cheek with his free hand.

Terror, pure in form, filled her senses and caused her to tremble, almost to the point of fainting. "Yeah," he continued, "even more than all this pretty hair on your pretty head, I like…" Slowly he lowered his mouth to her ear, licked it with his tongue and breathed his foul breath into it for a few seconds, then, so loud it even startled the men behind him, he shouted.

"FOOD!"

Laughing, the big man looked over his shoulder at the others and for a second they stared dumbfounded as if unsure how they were supposed to react, then one of them laughed too and the others followed.

The woman broke into hard sobbing, crying out loud, begging, "please, don't hurt me." The big man struck her across the face with a force that knocked her to the floor. Immediately she tasted the tang of blood in her mouth. Pointing a finger the man now towering over her screamed. "WOMAN! Don't ever talk unless I tell you to talk. You got that? Now get up and cook the boys and me some grub. And just remember, you do as I tell you to do, when I tell you. And when I call for you, you come running and remember this, when you speak to me, you call me Mr. Bracewell."

The men with him laughed again. He ignored them. "Now get your farmer's wife ass up and start cooking."

Suspended in a withdrawn world she did as she was told, not wanting to realize what all this horrible nightmare meant or wanting to think about its final moment.

While she cooked them stew and biscuits the men ransacked the house, ripping into cub-boards, trunks and closets. They found one pair of boots and Bracewell took them for himself. They were tight but he didn't care. One of the other men had returned to the barn and removed the boots from the woman's dead husband. She recognized them upon his return to the house and realized then, once and for all, her situation was hopeless.

Above the fireplace hung a rifle and six-gun, these too Bracewell kept for himself. Then, with a thrill of excitement, a bottle of whiskey was found.

By noon, the four men sat around the kitchen table tipsy and boisterous. Continuously, they threw sneering glances toward the woman who now sat silently in a chair near the stove. Always, she stared at the floor, never raising her head. Drunkenly they watched her, amusing themselves with lewd gestures and remarks. Within her own thoughts and memories, she was back in Boston with her family and husband.

Outside a light breeze blew across the dry yard and a swirl of sand danced off toward the barn. The wind fluttered a corner of the kitchen curtain and from the table came hushed whispers followed by waves of frightening laughter.

The woman remained silent, her long soft auburn hair falling about her shoulders - the hair her husband had so dearly cherished. But now she was wishing it were chopped short and uneven, in an ugly fashion, maybe then the men who watched her now would not desire her, would not find her attractive and leave her alone.

Fear was in her heart, and she was growing more aware of it. Her hands trembled so forcefully she could not control them even with conscious effort. Nevertheless, she had decided she would give them a fight and a taste of blood before they…

Still watching the floor at her feet, she heard chairs scrape against the plank floor and knew they were coming for her. There, in a state of mind so horrifying, like nothing she had ever known, for the first time in her life she wished she had a gun in her hand.

The strong arm pulled her forcefully from the chair and she caught him across the face with her nails coming away with flesh and blood. But she was no match. Easily the big man lifted her slamming her small figure hard onto the kitchen table.

Hands ripped at her dress and fumbled her roughly when the material was torn and gone. She kicked and pulled and scratched repeatedly but there were too many. Her screams seemed to go on endlessly, a desperate final cry for help, but none came.

With brutal savage force they took her, one after the other, and after the second and third man had had her she no longer amused them with her struggling and tears, but rather, lay inert and motionless, her cold distant eyes staring as if she were dead.

Again, she was far away in another time and another place, she still heard their faint muffled laughter and the sound of a snap or a buckle. And not at all to her surprise, the soft click. The six-gun kicked in the big man's hand with its bullet tearing through her abdomen and out the other side, burrowing into the rough-wood tabletop beneath her.

But below the barrel of the smoking gun the naked woman smiled at her last fading memory; a handsome young man from Boston, nervous and tongue-tied, asking for her hand.

The morning breeze felt cool and refreshing and it was this morning the Indian came out of his long sleep. His eyes opened and at first glance around him, his mind was blurred with confusion. The white people around him now were none of those that had attacked him, and he knew from the bandage on his side that these people had helped him. Seeing that the Indian's eyes were open, Labounty moved quickly to his side.

"My name is Labounty. Do you speak English?" The Indian did not reply but continued to stare. Labounty added, "I certainly hope you do since none of us speak Apache."

With calm, calculated silence the Indian studied the eyes of the white man beside him, reaching into his soul in search of the person within. And after a long while he was satisfied with what he saw, so he spoke.

"Yes, I speak your tongue."

Labounty smiled, explaining the situation. "We found you near the river where you had been shot." He pointed toward the bandage. "You have a bad infection, but I think you're on the mend."

The Indian placed his hand on the bandage. "You have removed the bullet then?"

"Yes. Fortunately it was lodged near where it went in and was easy to get at, otherwise who knows." Labounty saw a faint flicker of admiration in the Indian's eyes and then he smiled warmly.

"I am grateful. I owe you, my life." The Indian offered Labounty his hand and he took it. Labounty told him, "I appreciate that, but I can't take all the credit. They helped too." He glanced over his shoulder at Kay and Cub.

The woman and boy were sitting at the Indian's feet, and they smiled at him. Labounty introduced them.

"The woman is Kay, she is the one who bandaged you and helped with the removal of the bullet. I would not have been successful without her. The boy there goes by the name of Cub. He's been a big help in every way, sat by your side all the long hours your fever burned. He's a good man to have at your side."

The Indian looked at Kay and gave a warm nod. Then glanced into Cub's face, "Yes" he said to Labounty, "I can see it is as you say. His eyes tell me he is brave and proud like the Eagle."

Cub beamed, then looked over at Labounty for approval. The Indian smiled then looked again to Kay. "In my village there is a saying. 'A warrior's strength lies in the softness of his woman'. And a moment ago, when I looked into Labounty's eyes I saw great strength. I know now from where that strength comes from."

Labounty and Kay looked at one another; each began to speak but held their words instead. The Indian glanced into each of their faces, saying, "You are all my friends now, and my lodge shall always be open to you."

Labounty thanked him and replied, "It's my guess in just a few days you will be well enough to return to your people."

"Yes," the Indian said with urgency in his voice, "and that I return is most important."

Labounty said nothing of the fact he thought he knew who shot the Indian. The less said at this point the better. Besides, Apaches were not ones to speak of personal vendettas. So, he suggested the Indian lie back and rest.

Moving beside Kay, Labounty rolled a smoke not realizing he was being studied by the Indian. After lighting his cigarette, he stared soberly out over the desert. Lying comfortable as Labounty had suggested the Indian rolled onto his side and asked, "Tell me my friend, who is it you hide from?"

Surprised, Labounty turned to face him, deciding that maybe it was best to tell him everything.

"Well, I think it may be the same men who bushwhacked you. I have had a run-in with them already and this time I think they will come and stop at nothing."

The Indian sat up then, slowly, but showing no expression of the pain he must have felt just by moving. He smiled and Labounty felt a surge of calm reassurance. The Indian told him, "Then let them come Labounty, we will be waiting together."

And there, beneath a hot sun cooled by the soft desert breeze, a bonding was made, a friendship was born, one that would last forever.

The hours that followed passed pleasantly as the four talked. The Indian rested, eating and drinking in spurts. Slowly his strength was returning, and the infection was disappearing.

Several days and nights were spent camping there on the high brush along the river. It remained a risk, but one needed to take for the Indian's safe recovery.

Always at day the sun baked the earth, and they remained within the shade. At night the stars filled the sky and the moon glittered upon the water. And while they slept, both Labounty and the Indian remained subconsciously awake anticipating the arrival of Bracewell and his men. And although neither expressed it, each for their own reasons, found themselves waiting with a silent anticipation.

CHAPTER TWENTY

Four days were spent camped at the river and on the morning of the fifth day the Indian insisted he was well enough to ride and return to his people. Labounty consented but insisted they ride along, at least until they were sure he was past the danger stage and able to function on his own. Thankful, the Indian clasped Labounty's shoulder and smiled. "Yes," he said, "it is a good thing you do for me, and along the way, if we are lucky, then maybe this Bracewell and those with him will catch us. I would like that very much."

Labounty returned the smile knowing the Indian meant it, and in his heart knew that if or when it did happen, he would be a good man to have at his side.

The Indian's village lay miles away and a great distance from the river. Slowly, methodically, their horses sauntered through the wavering heat, pushing across open nothingness and away from the shade and coolness of the river, eastward in the direction of Gila Bend.

A little past noon they met a small band of Hopis. They told of three men that had been robbing and killing both Indians and white settlers and stealing horses and guns. The worst had been the killing of a white farmer and his wife, and how their tribe had been unjustly accused of the crime. The killers had run off all the stock, consisting of a couple of goats, a few chickens, and a milking cow. They had taken three horses; a good chestnut and two plow animals.

The milk cow had inadvertently wandered into one of the Hopi lodges. So caught up in the need for revenge, a band of white vigilantes hung the head of that family not even listening to their side. So angered now, the Hopi people talked of joining a faction wanting war.

Late in the afternoon Labounty shot a rabbit and in celebration they made camp early and cooked it. Along with bits of jerked beef and hardtack, Kay made a stew and served it with coffee. The Indian, who had asked that they call him Socorro, liked the taste of the stew very much and the taste of the coffee even more. When supper was over Labounty rolled a cigarette for his friend and together they sat smoking and talking.

In the firelight Kay cleaned the dishes and with Cub's help made ready their beds for the night. When all of this was done, she and Cub joined in the conversation. There had been idle talk of riding with the Indian to his village as his guests, and now, excited over the idea Cub talked to Socorro with enthusiasm, often asking questions without giving the Indian time to even answer.

"How long will it be, Socorro, before we reach your village? Do you think your people will like us; I mean we are different than you? How many boys will be there my age?"

The Indian smiled warmly at the youth's exuberance. "Do not be so eager, young one. To possess patience is as important a thing as the beating of your heart. It is not to my village that we ride, but rather to the village of a friend, a Puma friend. You will like the people there too".

Socorro turned his head to Labounty. My lodge is near the Painted Desert, in the territory of New Mexico. It is on business that I go to the Puma village, important business. There is talk of a unity of all Plains Indians, talk of war. I go now to counsel with a friend who has much influence over his brothers across this wide land. I am Jicarilla Apace. We are a proud people, willing to fight, but only after all other means have been tried. That is why I have been sent to speak on behalf of these other means. When you found me, I had just returned from my travels across the Mojave."

He took a draw from his cigarette and continued. " The people there had also been much restless, and I had reached them barely in time. So far, there have been only a few men I could not reason with. The worst was Jeronimo and his band. He is a Chiricahua and feels spiritually right in what he does." It is not easy to reason with a man who feels that what he does is right in his heart."

Socorro then looked turned back to Cub. "Labounty tells me that you can find the direction you wish to travel by use of the sun. And that you made your way across the desert on your own, making it nearly to the river."

Cub cut in excitedly, "Yeah, and after I rested, I could a made it the rest of the way too." He looked over at Labounty and smiled. "And after that, I could a made it on into Yuma… ifin' I'd wanted to."

The Indian, knowing what he was talking about, grasped his shoulder and laughed. "In my village, the young boys are given several tests to prove they are worthy of becoming a man. One such test is to run several miles in the heat of day with a mouthful of water. And this water they must not swallow but spit it out when they have reached their destination. Many fail that one." Cub's eyes were squinted in thought and the Indian held back a smile. "Another such test is to learn to dodge flying arrows, and in that one there is much danger."

Cub's eyes were glued to the Indian and in his boy-wondering mind he was lost to a vision of an Indian village with giant teepees and scattered cooking fires, with scores of small boys shooting bows and arrows and learning the skills of knife fighting. He pictured himself in buckskins made just for him and his hair long to his shoulders.

And so, the talk went until finally Cub lay with his head upon Kay's lap, sound asleep. Near the fire of red-glowing coals she laid him gently and covered him with a blanket. Then a lone coyote called into the night and the boy opened his sleepy eyes.

"Don't worry Kay," he told her, yawning, "there's nothing to be afraid of, us men are here."

The Indian was recovering quickly. The infection had diminished to little more than a reddened area and where the wound once was there was now a small scab. Carefully, Labounty had removed the stitches while Socorro watched with great interest. His strength had returned to near full and now he rode double with Cub, his shoulders back and face aglow with pride and dignity.

It was noon on the second day since leaving the river that they spotted the steady rise of dust in the far distance behind them. Through the glaring sun they watched, sitting their horses in silence. Then Labounty twisted to face the Indian. "Do you think it's them?"

"They are not Indian. These people ride in a group across the plains making the dust rise. If they were my kind and tracking prey, they would be riding far apart and not pushing their horses as these riders do. Yes, my friend, I think it is them." The Indian smiled. "Now come, let us find a place to greet them."

Reining the horses they turned and continued on, riding into the dancing heat waves and hot humid air, past the giant barrel cactus now standing tall around them. Single file, quiet and lost in thought, they rode on being watched suspiciously by perching buzzards and sunning Gila monsters. And not far behind rode four boisterous men who had no idea what would be waiting for them.

Up to now, Bracewell had been detestable in his actions, but after killing the farm family he had broken the final straw. No doubt remained now, when he caught up this time he would die.

It was late evening when the Indian raised his hand and stopped the others. "This is the place we will meet them", he said looking around, "but first, we must ride ahead and seek a safe place for the woman and boy. Once this is done, we will ride back and make ready".

The place the Indian had chosen for the attack was one of surprise to Labounty. It was without a good cover and there was nothing for concealment but a few cactus and small brush patches. And the ground lay covered with small, scattered stones. He had to admit, it was the last place four men would expect an ambush. Ambush! That was a word Labounty did not like. He had never had a desire to bushwack anyone. But Bracewell, he admitted, was not just anyone. He was a ruthless, cold-blooded killer. There was not a single thing about the man that gave even the slightest indication of decency. And because the others rode with him, they were no better.

Labounty considered the odds. Sure, there were four of them and only the Indian and himself, but in their favor would be the element of surprise. The Indian was now stronger and well on his way to full recovery, and the boy and Kay had been safely hidden away. Because Bracewell would not try and reason and would not let up until he had what he wanted, there was no other choice but to fight.

By the time Labounty and Socorro returned and dug two waist deep holes, one on either side of the trail, the stars were out and the night chill was upon the desert.

In the moonlight they brushed away their boot tracks, working their way back to the holes. The horses had been left tied a half-mile up on the trail hidden away as best as possible. A reasonable distance run, just in case they needed them. But the Indian smiled and assured Labounty they would not.

And so it was, through the night they waited. Darkness fell like a black sheet and light from the moon deformed the desert growth around them. The night air was chilling to a degree of moderate discomfort, but patiently they shivered away the hours waiting for the warm light of morning.

It was the Indian's guess the riders would reach them shortly after dawn, possibly before, but if his guess were right, it would not be before the yellowed sun showed all of itself in the morning sky.

With a blanket about his shoulders Labounty sat in the darkness, his mind adrift, lost in the place he cherished, in a mountain range of giant Sequoia and towering mountain peaks, a soft wind moaning and an even softer rain falling. He thought of the soothing warmth of a fire and of a small boy's smile. And he thought about Kay. He tried picturing himself a rancher or farmer with cattle and plowed fields and he tried picturing a family at his side. Rolling a cigarette, careful to conceal the match, he thought about himself. Wondered why he had never married.

He had always taken his career seriously and seldom had it crossed his mind to want a family. The railroad required constant traveling with long periods away; perhaps that had had a bearing on his thinking. A ranch, a good ranch, would require a woman, a special woman, one with courage and a willingness to work hard; one blessed with understanding, especially when it came to him. And children, every man should have a son to carry on his name, one to teach how to ride and rope and protect himself when a fight came along. And he would want a little girl too, with freckles that embarrassed her and eyes that sparkled with every bounce of her ponytails, one to someday walk down the aisle with a good man who would love and protect her and see to it grandchildren came along. "Yes," he thought to himself, "it was time he began thinking of such things."

It was the call of a quail that woke him. And in the gray shadows of predawn, a tint of yellow could be seen to the east. In thirty minutes, the morning sun would spill its welcomed light upon the land.

The quail that awoke him now flew over his head, followed by six others, calling out into the cold morning air. Shivering Labounty blew warm breath on his hands. Gazing through the gray coldness he tried spotting the Indian, but it was still too dark. Yawning, he pulled his blanket tightly around his shoulders.

Slowly but steadily the sun rose higher above the earth spilling light across the desert. Just before seven, Socorro moved to Labounty's side. "It is time. The riders will pass in only a few short minutes. Remain sill within the hole you have dug, and I will cover you with brush. Let them ride exactly between us before you fire. Remember, they are men of no good, of evil spirits, and will hurt the boy and woman if they get past us. Do not hesitate to shoot for it is important we surprise them. I will see you when it is over. Good luck my friend."

Socorro finished concealing Labounty then returned to his own spot, jumped quickly into his own hole and expertly pulled brush over himself.

The time had come. Guns ready, they waited.

CHAPTER TWENTY-ONE

This time there were six men. The Indian fired the first shot and knocked a rider from the saddle. In the same instant Labounty fired in suit and hell itself came to life.

Horses reared, screaming frightfully at the sudden confusion. The remaining riders out of instinct drew their guns but the crossfire in which they were caught was such that mere seconds marked the difference between life and death. They tried desperately to control their horses and at the same time spot a target at which to shoot, but none could be found.

The horse beside Bracewell went down and its rider cursed aloud. Bracewell's own mount reared and took a stray round in the haunches. With great force the animal struck the ground and sent him rolling. Bullets kicked up dirt all around him.

Gunfire was echoing across the desert in a loud terrifying sound without end. Dirt and dust rose and swirled about the frightened horses and men yelled in total confusion. Labounty and Socorro levered and shot their rifles as fast as humanly possible. A lone horse without a rider galloped past Labounty's hole but he continued to fire.

Then his rifle was empty. Throwing it down he grabbed his pistol…
but he never fired it. As suddenly as the shooting had begun it ended. And
now an unsettling quietness accompanied by settling dust, dead men, three
dead Horses and a silence filling the void between himself and Socorro.

Remaining cautiously in their holes the two men studied the throng
of bodies. Three horses lay dead, one whose rider lay spread-eagle across
its neck, another whose rider had fallen parallel to its body face down, a
third horse lay atop the legs of a man with a chunk of forehead missing, a
forth body lay close to Socorro's hole and a fifth lay down the trail where
he had tried to run but did not make it. As for the sixth man… he was
unaccounted for and Labounty swore under his breath, of course it was
Bracewell.

The Indian, covered by Labounty, left his hole and quickly checked
the bodies. There had been no one left alive except for Bracewell. Off to
the east through a brush patch his tracks cut into the dirt at a dead run.

Socorro walked over to where Labounty was climbing out of his
hole. His face serious. The Indian told him. "The big one, he is gone. His
tracks lead off that way. Go to the girl and boy, I will hunt him."

Out of the hole now Labounty looked into the Indian's face.

"No Socorro." He spoke the Indian's name firmly but with respect.
"This man has caused great embarrassment to both our people. He has
already killed several of them, one of which was a woman and even now
his reason for tracking us was to get to Kay. He nearly killed me once. It is
I who should track him."

The Indian studied Labounty for a long time, saying finally.

"And so, it shall be my friend. I then am he who will go and wait
with the boy and woman."

After retrieving his horse Labounty began following the tracks. For
almost two miles Bracewell's stride had been wide - a strong, continuous
run. Another quarter mile on and he found where he had stopped to rest.

Frequently he ran through brush patches making it difficult or
impossible to follow by horseback, forcing Labounty to ride around

checking for exits. But there were few places the man could hide and wait in ambush. Cactus towered in places and clumps of twisted sage roots hugged the hard ground. There were no trees within miles and the nearest mountain range stood at least a full day's ride away.

Eyes alert, Labounty reasoned. If Bracewell was smart and thinking fast, he had with him a rifle, pistol and canteen. The small amount of water would last only a short time. If the man wanted to try and out distance him then he would fall short, he was on foot. That left only one choice, ambush.

The air had nearly lost its morning coolness and the heat of day was coming alive. Labounty stopped and drank long from his canteen. He had learned long ago that it was better to drink water in the cool of morning and not in the heat of day. After watering his horse, he moved on. Behind him buzzards were already gathering in the sky and by now the Indian was with Cub and Kay. That thought consoled him and helped him concentrate solely on tracking Bracewell.

First, he heard the report of the bullet leaving the muzzle than his horse collapsed beneath him. It fell almost instantly, deadweight, and lay there on its side, kicking. Labounty rolled quickly the moment he hit the dirt. Gun in hand he lay still, alert and observing the surroundings.

The animal's chest rose and fell wildly as it tried to rise but could not. Then it made a strange noise and fell silent. Quickly Labounty crawled behind its dead carcass as bullets began kicking up the dirt around him.

Not far ahead he caught the faint glitter of a rifle barrel and pulled his own out of its boot. Taking careful aim, he fired three rounds into the brush where he had seen the glitter. Bracewell himself didn't stop firing until he had used up every round in his Winchester.

Labounty guessed him to have no reloads. He would be left now with only his handgun and he was out of range for it. So, rising to his feet Labounty began zigzagging on the run where Bracewell lay. He heard the handgun fire repeatedly. Four times it erupted before Labounty threw a slug of his own, firing from the hip. He was gaining rapidly on Bracewell's location and could see him plainly now.

It was after he had fired his last two shots, emptying his six-gun that Bracewell rose realizing his mistake, with no time to reload he knew there was nothing left to do except to kill Labounty with his bare hands. So, he charged him.

They crashed into each other with violent impact. Like mad dogs they tore at one another, fighting to the death in a lonely land where no help would ever come. There would be no ultimatums, no rules, and no holds barred - only win or die. Then they tumbled.

Dust rose about them as they fought there in the dirt. Somewhere Bracewell came up with a knife and Labounty grabbed the strong wrist just in time. They rolled over once, twice, three times. The heat in the sky mounted and their breath began growing short. Then Labounty's arm gave out and he rolled his head to the side quickly. The knife blade came down with tremendous force grazing his cheek. Blood surfaced and rolled down his face. Labounty threw a left and caught Bracewell's jaw, stunning him. The killer groaned and rolled free, his mind clouded with dizziness and pain.

Quickly Labounty rose to his feet and threw a kick, but Bracewell moved, and it missed. Two powerful arms wrapped around his legs and Labounty lost balance. He slammed hard to the ground, nearly losing his breath. But he managed to break Bracewell's grip and climb quickly back on his feet once more.

Sometime during the fight, the knife had been dropped but neither had even a second to search for it. A weighted blow crashed against his ear and Labounty felt great pain, it reddened and began swelling. Bracewell was a skilled fighter and a powerful man, no one at all to underestimate. He swung again, but this time Labounty let it pass over then came up with all he had under the man's chin. The force of the blow lifted Bracewell completely off the ground before he fell. He was stunned momentarily and Labounty took advantage. Straddling him, he immediately raised his fist for another powerful blow - but the sudden roar of a rifle stopped him cold, and he turned.

The small band of Indians sat their ponies with rifles pointed. There were seven, traveling light and painted for war. No one spoke at first, and the desert fell silent as dust slowly settled about the two men. Both Labounty and Bracewell lost all interest in their fight and slowly rose to their feet.

Then one of the braves made a motion with his rifle barrel and spoke something in his own tongue, two other Indians left their ponies instantly and approached them.

First, they bound their hands behind them then tied a rope securely around their necks, linking them together with a six-foot distance and a long lead rope of eight or ten feet to be used to pull them along. Once the two warriors returned to their ponies something else was said in their language and the entire party laughed at the two bound men.

With a light click and a shake of the reins the horses started off - the slack in the rope was taken up quickly and the two men were jerked forward, nearly losing their balance. Cruelly, they were pulled along, forced to walk at a near run behind the ponies, knowing the gruesome results should they stumble.

The heat was dreadfully hot now, for the sun was high. The air around them lingered, lacking any form of humidity. About their necks the rope see-sawed as they walked, and from the onset, the skin beneath had begun to rub raw.

Expressionlessly the two men pushed on, struggling to keep up with the pace of the horses but careful to hide all signs of pain. To do so would be to show weakness and weakness now would only mean an early death. Both knew there was chance of escape so long as they endured.

Hour after hour they trailed behind the ponies, legs tired and lungs burning from the dry heat. In their hearts they knew there would come no help. Labounty thought of Socorro, but he was on a peace mission, trying to prevent war, and this party would never listen. So, Labounty thought, if they were to live, they must find their own way out.

Beneath the blistering sun they treaded, tiny, scattered stones tearing at the soles of their boots and making each step an awkward and often clumsy effort. Occasionally a brave would turn and stare, each time with a look of pride and eagerness on their face.

Where they were being taken Labounty had no idea. He did guess it would be a village somewhere nearby, so that all who lived there could share in the glory of their screams during torture. If so, he thought, then he would do his best to disappoint them by enduring as long as possible. If he were destined to die this way, then he would do it honorably.

CHAPTER TWENTY-TWO

Socorro had begun to worry. Several hours had passed since leaving Labounty and he should have been back long ago. Because the man he tracked was on foot and Labounty on horseback and the terrain mere open desert, it should have taken only a short time to run down the man called Bracewell.

There was concern on the face of the others too. Kay paced and Cub questioned the Indian, demanding to know of Labounty's welfare. When Socorro's could not satisfy the youngster's need for encouragement, the boy stormed off to his horse determined to ride after his friend.

Smiling with admiration the Indian stopped him. And after placing both hands on the boy's shoulders, he kneeled saying' "Someday you will grow into a great warrior. Labounty is fortunate to call you, his friend. I myself will go and search for him. It is important you stay here and protect the woman," he looked at Kay and winked so that Cub could not see, then looked back, "there are many dangers in this land and she will need a warrior to watch over her."

Cub's face grew thoughtful. Straightening his shoulders, he looked over at Kay, then back at Socorro. "I reckon you're right; she is a girl."

Looking at the Indian Kay raised her eyebrows, wondering if she should feel insulted or flattered. Either way she smiled warmly inside.

After reminding them of the importance of staying hidden within the thick brush, Socorro removed all signs of tracks and rode out in search.

Labounty could be lying in the dirt somewhere dying with Bracewell footloose and on the run, but the Indian believed that highly unlikely. His friend had left knowing full well the odds and the ways of the man he tracked. So, he thought, the reason for his friend not returning had to be something else, something unexpected.

In just a short distance, stopping his horse Socorro slid to the ground. Labounty's horse laid dead and a few hundred feet to the right, the ground was badly torn up by two men on foot; it was obvious they had struggled with one another. And just outside of what had been their fighting space, the tracks of seven unshod ponies had made an outer circle around them. What had happened required little guesswork.

The Indian looked up at the sun then back toward the direction he had just come. He considered the situation only a short time, then remounted and rode off, following the tracks of the unshod ponies…and his friend.

The air about him was hot and sticky with discomfort. But that it bothered him even in the slightest he gave no indication. Before him, miles of heat waves shimmered - deforming the earth and creating deceiving pools of cool water.

Socorro had no way of telling which band of Indian had taken the men captive. He was sure, however, that it had not been Jeronimo, for had it been him he would have found both men dead.

This was Pima land, but at present, they remained friendly. Perhaps it had been Blackfoot, he had heard they were coming down from the northern lands and raiding.

Sweat ran down Socorro's back. The terrain about him was barren of shade and there was no breeze. So far, the tracks were not difficult to follow and that was good. However, he did worry for Labounty, for he knew the war party would not let him ride and the sun was terrible in its warmth with death lingering within its heat.

The woman and boy would be safe if they remained where they were. To venture out could mean running into another war party. He had told them that he would return before nightfall of the next day and that if he did not, then they were to travel with caution to the river and follow it to Yuma.

Choosing his own pace, Socorro followed the tracks diligently. How far the war party intended to travel he did not know, nor could he guess. He could only hope they would stop for the night and make camp. If they did, and despite his fear of dying during the dark hours, it would be then that he would have to overtake them. There would be no chance during the daylight hours.

Riding throughout the day Socorro maintained his slow deliberate pace. By the time the shadows had gathered in the late afternoon he stopped and cursed in his own tongue. The tracks he had been following, so far with ease, were suddenly gone. The war party had begun covering them. Why, he could not be sure. It was possible they had spotted him following, but he did not think so. For if that were true, they would have waited and attacked him in ambush. It had to be they were nearing their camp and acting out of precaution. To Socorro that idea made sense, so it was that he chose to believe.

Less than three more hours of daylight remained and if he was to find Labounty, a minute could not be lost. Reining his horse, he began moving in small, looping circles, always working outward with each completed pass, searching for a sign that may have been overlooked.

He did this until at last, the final speck of light vanished, and darkness made way for a few, scanty stars. The night air about him was cool but before morning he knew it would grow much colder.

With reluctance he dropped from his horse, there would be no more searching that night. At daylight he would continue, and if the Great Spirit were with him, he would find a sign, for finding a sign was now the only hope his friend possessed.

With a blanket about his shoulders Socorro sat upon the ground staring at the stars. There was but a half-moon and the temperature was dropping rapidly. The few stars that were showing were cold like the night around him, and even now when he exhaled, he could see his breath in the dim moonlight.

In a soft voice the Indian began to hum. Tonight, there would be no fire, not for warmth or on which to cook. His enemies could be close, and the comfort of a glowing fire was not worth the risk of being spotted. If he were to save his friend, he would need the element of surprise.

A coyote called from somewhere out in the darkness, and he stopped his humming to listen. It called again and another answered. Satisfied it was the call of animals, he dropped the blanket from his shoulders, letting it fall to the ground behind him. Gracefully he rose to his feet and raised his open arms toward the starry sky.

He began to chant. And as he chanted, his mind told the Gods of a man brave and caring, of a friend who had saved his life and without concern for himself was now risking his own to help a small boy and a woman.

A long time Socorro chanted, praying to the Great Spirit for help. And as the long hours passed, daylight slowly inched across the world toward him, until finally it chased away the stars and the moon, surrendering to an overpowering light.

CHAPTER TWENTY-THREE

Labounty had been watching the blue sky grow gradually lighter. An eastern storm was rolling slowly in their direction. Several times he had caught a glimpse of lightning and heard the distant rumbling of thunder.

He welcomed it though, for the storm would prove a triple blessing. First it would delay their torture. Secondly, it could possibly aid them in their escape. And thirdly it would help to cool their red burned skin.

Labounty guessed they had traveled seven or eight miles since their capture, moving steadily through the night stopping only twice to rest. Now, ahead perhaps five or six miles in the approach of morning, he could see the dark remnants of rock formations. He was confident that was their destination.

By the time the sun streaked the horizon they had covered the five miles and stood in a small Indian camp. Women, children and barking dogs excited by the commotion had gathered to celebrate the return of their warriors.

By now daylight was but minutes away and with it would come the much-needed opportunity to rest. Both men were drained physically, fatigued to a dangerous level.

Upon their arrival both had been stripped to the waist and tied spread-eagle to ground stakes. Their necks and wrists were now raw and swollen and even without the stinging bite of the rope, blood seeped through the opened skin.

The camp was not large and had been set up on a temporary basis. Nine teepees sat huddled to the north just beyond their heads. Obviously not concerned with being discovered, the entire encampment burned with night fires and all who occupied it danced in celebration of their war party's spoils.

The night air was warming but Labounty still shivered some. Testing his bonds, he pulled with great strength but to no avail. There would be no breaking free.

Bracewell tied to his left looked over at him.

"I got to tell you Labounty, this ain't the way I intended to go. Some little whorehouse in San Francisco would have been to my choosing, dying in bed with a cute little fancy just begging me to…"

"Shut your mouth Bracewell." Labounty snapped.

Bracewell laughed. "Well will you listen to you. I suppose you'd rather die in a church listening to a preacher. I got to tell you Labounty, if I do die here, I only regret two things. First, I never tasted your red headed lady friend. And second these filthy red devils interrupted us too soon. I would have enjoyed killing you."

Labounty gave no reply and a cold silence fell between them.

Side by side they stared silently into an ever-brightening sky. Gray stretched storm clouds floated freely above. Amid the singing and dancing and beating of drums somewhere above their heads, wind whistled through the camp.

The two men lay red from sun and rope burns, sore, tired, and still fighting some chill from the wind and fatigue. They had no way of knowing, but Socorro lay watching them from a nearby ridge. Rolling onto his back he thanked the Great Spirit for hearing his prayer and now asked for one more favor, to help free his friend from those who planned to kill him.

Long before the Sun rose high, a light rain began, quickly turning into a mad stinging downpour. Both men turned their heads to avoid its powerful bombardment. The droplets felt icy and at first took their breath away. Tribunal fires quickly died and all, but a single guard scrambled for their lodges.

The downpour was what Socorro had been waiting for. Silently he left the ridge making way toward the camp. The corral was his first stop. There he carefully led each horse away, turning it loose and running down into the open desert. Only one did he retain and walk back to where his own mount was tied. When finished he returned once again to the area of the camp.

The rain continued to fall hard, slamming noisily onto the ground. Soon the desert floor would be wet with a slushy surface. And so long as the rain persisted there would be no tracks for which their enemies could follow.

He would have waited until night with everyone sound asleep, but because of the hard rain, this made it a good time as well. For no one would expect a plunderer to creep into their camp during daylight. Besides, to take advantage of the harsh storm was wise, since by morning it would be gone and the earth would dry up quickly, leaving tracks to follow.

The guard sat near the two men on the ground with a deer hide blanket over his head and shoulders. For Socorro working his way behind was no problem. With the downpour all sound was lost to the rain.

Labounty and Bracewell's shivering was growing worse beneath the cold hammering torrent. To distract his mind Labounty closed his eyes and thought of Cub and Kay. He was totally unaware of Socorro's presence, for had he have known, that alone would have warmed him with hope.

Knowing the rain would wash away all tracks Labounty had all but given up hope that his Indian friend would find them if in fact he had even begun to search at all. And now, even if, or when, he found them, by that time it would be too late.

On the good side, the boy would be in good hands with his Indian friend, and he was confident he would see to it both Cub and Kay got to Yuma safely. Cub was a good kid and possessed great potential. Labounty wanted to be there when the youngster met his relatives for the first time. It could turn out they would not be right for him. And if so he himself had friends, married friends, couples who might be interested in taking on the responsibility of a small boy.

Labounty closed his eyes with surprise at himself, his own house was plenty large enough, perhaps it would be…he stopped himself. No, he thought, that would never work. The youngster needed a woman's touch too, not the one-sided upbringing of a man alone. For balance and stability, he needed both a mother and father figure.

His thoughts shifted to Kay. She was quite a woman and certainly caught in an unfortunate situation. Yes, it had become his personal intention, should she agree, to take her to his lawyer and find a legal way out of her dilemma. Undoubtedly, good representation would be the key to righting such injustice.Personally, he did indeed hope she would except the offer.

Behind his closed eyes he imagined her sitting beside him now, the touch of her warm hand chasing away the terrible cold. He could see her smile and red cascading hair and even amid the stale smell of wet earth and drifting smoke from drowned tribunal fires, he imagined the fresh-soft fragrance of her skin. Under his breath he whispered her name. "Kay"!

When Socorro slammed the handle of his knife against the guard's head he fell forward like a bag of sand, splashing into a small puddle of water. Moving hastily to Labounty's side he cut his bonds while watching through the falling rain toward the camp. Labounty was speechless; and thankful!

Bracewell watched with big enthusiastic eyes, waiting impatiently for his turn to be cut loose. The moment Labounty was free, Socorro pulled him to his feet. Bracewell stared up at them and it dawned then, they intended to leave him. Making a face he cursed them both.

"You sons-of-bitches." Loud as possible he began to yell, his voice slicing sharply through the down poor. "Hey, they're getting away you red-skinned bastards, they're…" His yelling ended abruptly however when Socorro's knife handle came down against the side of his head.

From the teepees there came a sudden great commotion with shadowy warriors appearing amidst the hard-falling rain. There was finger pointing and yelling.

Socorro and Labounty turned and began running. To make it to the horses would now be their only hope of escape. Water splashed wildly beneath their feet and mud flew in a mad fury. Behind them several braves followed at a great run firing a volley of rounds through the rain in their direction.

The horses were not far but neither were the runners behind them. The heavy rain hid much of the surroundings and Socorro knew there could be no room for error. They must make it to the horses on the first try, and even then, perhaps their pursuing enemies were too close and there would not be time to mount and ride off. If they were tackled before reaching the horses there would be no getting awayg, for there were far too many warriors to fight.

The rain stung their skin. The way to the awaiting horses was through a long brush patch, up the side of a small slope and on to the very ridge where Socorro had laid watching.

They were now nearly through the patch coming onto the slope. A bullet flew by and Labounty heard it zing past his ear. Then they were through and starting up the incline. Behind them the braves were closing, with the continuous echo of rifle fire and excited voices.

The mud made climbing awkward and clumsy. Bullets were striking all around them and it was only by fate they were not struck. The air was cold, and the rain felt like falling globules of ice.

Then Socorro slipped, stumbling to the ground and sliding down the slope. As he slid, he yelled to Labounty, urgency in his voice; "Ahead, straight as you go, the horses are tied, run quickly." Then they were on top of him, six of them, while two continued after Labounty.

The rain continued to fall in a hard downpour. Labounty reached the horses, but he did not mount, instead, with speed and planned timing he grabbed the mane of the one nearest and as a point of balance pulled himself half up, then kicked outward catching one brave square in the face. He went down hard and stayed there lying face first in the mud. Then the second warrior tackled him with great force. They slammed hard into the soaked ground, rolling amid the mud and water puddles. They fought, but there was really no match. Labounty threw the first blow, and the warrior was stunned. He followed with two more and the Indian was out cold.

Socorro's fight was worse. A knife had come up in his hand, and with it he killed one brave. Another he disabled with a deep slash across the face. Four were left and as he struggled, he knew there would be no chance of overpowering them all.

Then out of the blackness Labounty flew through the air, his feet catching one of the four directly in the chest sending him flying down the steep muddy slope. He himself crashed hard to the ground and two braves piled on top of him, one had a knife. Socorro was left now with only one brave with which to struggle. Both he and his opponent had a knife and together they rolled over and over while slowly sliding down the slope.

Labounty threw a right round house and struck an ear. The slash of a knife hand came out of the hard rain, and he blocked it, but barely in time. Then he felt a hard object smash against his head. Bright stars flashed before his eyes, and he sank into an unconscious sleep. With Labounty out, Socorro was soon over-powered by the Blackfeet worriers, and although now fewer in number, they chattered in the hard rain, boasting now of three prisoners instead of two.

CHAPTER TWENTY-FOUR

When Labounty awoke the bright sun caused him to squint. As before he was staked to the ground beside Bracewell, only this time his Indian friend lay to his right.

Socorro looked over at him, appreciation in his voice. "Among my people you would be considered a brave and respected warrior. They would honor you for coming back to save me from my enemies. But I my friend, think you are crazy like a dumb man". He grinned. "But thank you."

Bracewell cut in with sarcasm, "I think I'm going to cry. You both deserve every bit of being here with me. You were going to leave me to die alone at the hands of these red skinned bastards."

Labounty looked over at him. "You deserve to be left. I never thought I'd say this about another human being Bracewell, but you don't deserve to even share the air good people breathe. Bracewell snapped back. "And you do Mr. High and Mighty? You are no better than me".

Labounty looked up into the sky then back at Bracewell.

"At least I know the meaning of compassion and respect for the rights of others. Let me tell you something, the things we do in life always come back to us. Just like the good book says, 'we reap what we sow'. And you better hope the good Lord shows pity on your evil soul."

Bracewell laughed out loud. "Cut the preacher crap Labounty, it's shit. If I go to Hell, I'll just take over that's all". He shook his head then laid it to rest on the ground.

There was an agreeable silence between them. The sun was hot on their bare chests, and it slowly shrunk the leather bindings about their wrists, tightening painfully. Labounty's head hurt but he tried ignoring it while working his fingers.

Their situation looked bleak. Two guards stood watch now and no one was left to rescue them. Kay and Cub were on their way to Yuma by now, and for that he was thankful. Likely, with Bracewell here with them their journey would be a safe one.

It was unfortunate Socorro would die before completing his mission of peace. For not only was he a good man, but a powerful influence and could have prevented useless bloodshed. Bracewell's dying on the other hand would be an improvement to mankind. As for himself, Labounty grinned. At least his last mountain excursion lacked nothing less than excitement.

At noon the three were cut loose and their hands retied behind their backs. They were then taken to a teepee and made to sit on the dirt floor opposite an aged and frail looking Indian with long, thinning gray hair. Dressed in colorful beaded buckskins the old man appeared as someone with authority, no doubt the Blackfeet chief. His face was heavily creased with age lines and greatly wrinkled, and from the left side of his hair hung one single feather. His expression was one of seriousness yet in his old eyes Labounty saw flickers of both wisdom and compassion.

In silence the men sat sober, their minds fearing what lay ahead and their hearts coming to grips with the idea that soon death would come to claim their souls.

The old man looked first at Socorro and asked if he could speak English. When he nodded yes that became the tongue of choice for the old Chief spoke it as well, and wanted all to understand what was said. Eyes remaining on Socorro the old Indian began, his english clear.

"You are Apache, and they are great warriors." The old man's voice was soft, and he chose his words slowly. "My people say you fought bravely at the slope on which you were taken. When you first entered our camp to free your friend," he looked at Labounty then back to Socorro, "you did not kill my guard and you could have easily. Such a deed speaks loudly and creates an opening into your heart. The warrior who you killed on the slope you did so in battle and so he died in honor. You have not disgraced us and that is to your favor."

When the old man turned his eyes on Labounty he stared a long time before speaking. Their eyes remained locked. Then he said. "You were caught fighting with this man," the chief glanced at Bracewell then back again to Labounty, "why was this fight?"

Not removing his eyes, Labounty spoke firmly. "This man has brought great shame among my people. He has done many bad things. At first it was my attempt to take him to jail to be judged fairly by our law. But he escaped from me and while away he murdered and raped, and this terrible thing was blamed on the Hopi people and unjustly they were punished."

Bracewell cut in. "Chief, that son-of-a-bitch is lying to you. He's the one who murdered and raped. It was me who was taking him to jail."

Socorro wanted to speak, to defend his friend, to reinforce the truth of Labounty's words, but it was not the Indian way. He would not speak unless asked to do so.

The old chief looked calmly at Bracewell. "You speak to me out of turn and in haste and anger." The old man paused but did not take his eyes from Bracewell. After a long time of studying his face he added, "If I chose to believe that it is you who is the good man and him the bad, what would you have me do with him?"

Bracewell looked over at Labounty. "Kill him."

"And you?" the old Chief said looking to Labounty, "if I chose to believe you are the Goodman and he the bad one, what would you have me do with him?"

Staring into the Indian's eyes, Labounty told him. "I would have you turn him over to me and I would finish taking him to our law. I am sure he would be found guilty and hanged; that would be the right thing to do."

Bracewell began to speak again but the old Indian raised his hand and silenced him. Then he looked once more at Socorro.

"We, my people, know that you were on a journey of peace. We too want peace across our land, but many times the words of the white-eyes are not true. We who are only a few have chosen war, but the thing you do is good. The whites are many and soon will drive us all from our homes and, like many before us, send us off to places far away and strange to us. In our hearts we know that peace is the choice of most of our people and if the spirits are kind, then a day will come upon us when all men of every color will live in such peace. In my heart you are my brother and have gained my respect. You are free to go and with you I send the open door to my lodge."

Socorro felt relief, but in his heart, there remained a heavy burden. In silence he waited to hear the outcome of his friend. The Chief spoke to both Labounty and Bracewell together.

"One of you is a good warrior and one is a bad. It is not for me to choose but is a thing left to the spirits to decide. Tonight, before the sun sleeps you will once again fight. One will die and one will live, the one who lives will be set free. It is the belief of our people that darkness is strong, and goodness is strong. It is the acts of a man that tell us which strength lives in his heart. So go now, eat and rest, and pray to your God you are that one who walks in goodness.

CHAPTER TWENTY-FIVE

At 5:30 a hundred or more Indians, men, women and children, gathered to form a huge circle; some sat and others stood. And centered within this circle, a single steel-headed tomahawk lay on the ground glistening beneath the remaining bright searing sun. The on lookers milled and chatted excitedly, waiting patiently for the fight to begin.

Socorro, now a free man stood among the crowd, his heart heavy as he silently prayed to the Great Spirit. The ground within the circle was dry, baked by the days burning rays of sunlight. It was upon this ground blood would soon flow and so he prayed it would not be Labounty.

Across from him the crowd broke apart making a walkway through which both men were brought and stood. They were positioned facing one another. The old chief entered the circle behind them, and silence fell over the crowd. Eyes turned upon him and all listened with eagerness. The ancient leader spoke first to his people in Blackfoot then changed to English. Looking always one to the other, he told Labounty and Bracewell.

"Now is time of truth. Look to see past your muscle and blood and into the heart of the man you are. It is from there you will pull out a true warrior's strength. There are good spirits and bad spirits, each help their own kind. That is why the rain falls on the good and the not good. It is our belief when the final speck of dust has settled, and all has been done that can be done- good shall win over bad. When I drop the feather," he pulled the hanging feather from his hair and held it out in front of him. "When it drops you must stand still and not run for the tomahawk until the feather has struck the ground. He who runs before the feather touches will be killed before he reaches the center of the circle, such haste will speak as words of guilt. Now prepare in your heart for battle."

Labounty and Bracewell were positioned apart and facing one another, north and south within the circle. The Chief and his feather walked to the center. Both men stiffened with tension, watching the feather in the old man's hand. The crowd was breathless and around them the circle remained quiet and still. The sun threw down its burning rays and sweat was already glistening on the chest of both men. This time there would be no interruption, no interference, and no help from anyone. It would be muscle against muscle, strength against strength, man against man. Soon one would lay dead and the other given his freedom.

Glaring at the feather Labounty wondered what would be the outcome? He had lived long enough to learn fate was often unfair or at least appeared that way to the limited understanding of man. Many times, during the war he had seen evil overwhelmingly subdue good. The old Indian's wisdom was correct, rain did fall on good and bad alike. "Yes, it was said that, in the end good would win over evil - but that was the outcome of the war, this was but a small battle in that war, thus making the outcome unpredictable.

Bracewell was strong and cunning and a skilled fighter, no one to underestimate. And to him killing came easy. He was a hard enemy and the bigger man, standing a head taller. But Labounty believed their strength to be equal and he himself had fought long and hard during the war where he had done his share of killing too. But unlike Bracewell, killing to him did not come so easy. And here, he could not let that feeling get in the way.

The feather fell from the old Indian's fingers. Slowly it floated downward, drifting calmly and peacefully toward the hard-baked earth. Both men stood their ground, wanting to charge, wanting to be the first to reach the Tomahawk, but each harnessed their eagerness, remembering the warning of the old man. So, eyes anxious, minds filled with unbearable tension, they followed the floating feathers's descent.

Seemingly the world had become a place of slow motion, nothing moved, nothing existed but the slow, tedious fall of the feather. Unhurriedly it drifted upon the wings of the soft breeze now sweeping the circle of staring eyes. Floating downward with ease, it turned and spun antagonizing all who stood watching. Sweat streaked the faces of both men and the salt bit at their eyes, but they dared not blink.

Then it hit.

CHAPTER
TWENTY-SIX

Both men bolted for the Tomahawk wanting desperately to be the first to reach it; the one who did would have the advantage. From the crowd arose excited cheers and yelling… and so the race for life began!

Both reached the weapon at the same instant. Neither had time to grab it, for flesh and bone collided. Muscle and raw strength fell hard to the ground and like two snarling dogs each went for the other's throat. Dust rose within the circle as they rolled.

With one hand on Labounty's throat, Bracewell used the other to gouge at his eyes. Flesh tore just below his right eyebrow and Labounty felt blood spill down his face. His vision would now be impaired.

Labounty countered with a solid right and struck Bracewell just above the right ear, a smacking sound was heard, and the pain of the blow sent Bracewell rolling free of him. Labounty rose quickly to his feet as did Bracewell.

They circled one another cautiously. The glistening Tomahawk lay to their left a good six feet away. Each watched it with the corner of their eye. Each wanted it, for each desired to kill the other with it.

Bracewell charged catching Labounty in the midsection with his head and both men went down. As they fell, Labounty flipped Bracewell over his head and sent him rolling away - then moving quickly, he scrambled to the Tomahawk and rose with it in his hand. From the crowd came loud cheers. Bracewell was back on his feet too.

The head of the Tomahawk glittered beneath the sunlight. Labounty swung a wide arc and Bracewell ducked, letting it fly over his head. With great speed he moved backwards, careful to maintain his balance.

The cut below Labounty's eye continued to seep blood and already the eye was beginning to swell shut. He swung the Tomahawk again. This time it caught Bracewell across the chest, and he yelled as skin opened and blood surfaced, racing down the chest to his waist. Again, the crowd of on-looking Indians cheered.

The hot sticky air made breathing difficult. Both men were tiring quickly, their strength flowing from their bodies like the heat waves rising from the hot desert floor.

With heaving chests, they continued to circle. Labounty swung the axe again- it flew past Bracewell and that was what he had been waiting for. With great speed he tackled Labounty and they both went down. Again, they rolled over with Bracewell straddling Labounty and clutching the wrist holding the Tomahawk. Their grips were equally matched. Labounty swung a powerful blow with his free hand but missed. Bracewell returned with a blow of his own, striking the swelling cut just above Labounty's eye. Blood splattered and Labounty groaned against the pain, dropping the Tomahawk. Bracewell swung again, but Labounty moved his head and it missed.

Rolling free, Bracewell grabbed the axe and scrambled to his feet. So did Labounty, wiping blood out of his eye and watching Bracewell carefully. Again, they circled. Then Bracewell swung the axe and Labounty ducked. He swung again and still yet another miss forcing Labounty to move quickly backwards avoiding another killing swing.

Bracewell was smiling, liking the feel of having the upper hand. Then Labounty dropped to his side and kicked Bracewell's feet out from under him. The man went down hard, crashing heavily onto the ground, momentarily he was stunned and gasped for his breath.

Labounty climbed to his feet and Bracewell made it to his knees. With all the strength he could muster, Labounty caught him under the chin with a kick, his jaw snapped and the momentum sent Bracewell flying onto his back. The Tomahawk flew from his hand and Labounty retrieved it quickly.

Staggering as he stood, and breathing laboriously, he watched as Bracewell lay on the ground moaning, teetering with unconsciousness. From the crowd came a thunderous cheer followed by a unanimous chant in Blackfoot. Labounty did not know the word, but he understood its meaning.

With a face twisted in pain Bracewell blinked repeatedly, bringing himself back to his full senses. When he was there, he stared up at Labounty and lifting up his hands told him above the nosy crowd. "That's it, I can't go on. You win. But at least let me die like a man in front of these red-skinned bastards. Let me be on my feet while you do it." Bracewell stared, waiting for the answer. "Please." He added, "I may be worthless in your eyes, but I do have my pride."

Labounty looked down at him. To kill a man like this was against everything he believed in. Yet it had to be done. Only one of them could leave the circle alive and perhaps this moment, this outcome, was the planned destiny for the both.

Reaching down Labounty took his hand and pulled him up. The moment Bracewell was on his feet and balanced, he smiled. "You fool!" Then he threw a handful of dry parched dirt into Labounty's face. The pain was instant, and he dropped the Tomahawk to clutch his eyes. Automatically he moved backwards, rubbing desperately at the stinging pain and fighting for vision. He had but seconds to clear his sight.

The crowd had ceased with the chant and now yelled angrily into the circle. While Labounty rubbed frantically at his eyes Bracewell approached him laughing, the Tomahawk was raised high above his head with the top of Labounty's skull his target.

Socorro yelled and began to run into the circle but the old Chief stopped him with a stern voice.

"NO, it must be. The spirits will decide."

Then Bracewell was there, and he swung the axe with all of his strength, a power that would tare through Labounty's skull and burry the blade deep into his brain. With only a second of vision between waves of pain Labounty saw it, quickly pivoting he threw up an arm beneath Barcewell's wrist to stop the falling blade. The deadly blow was avoided but the deflection of the axe tore a chunk of flesh from his shoulder, Labounty cried out as the group of watchers screamed angrily.

Bracewell lost his footing and dropped the Tomahawk for balance to stay on his feet. He recovered quickly but there was not time to retrieve the axe. Labounty charged him and once again they collided. Each grabbed the throat of the other.

On their feet and face to face, they stood groaning, teeth gritted. Their muscles bulged and veins protruded. With brute strength each struggled to crush the throat of the other. Once again, and for what would be the last time, the crowd began to chant.

Faces red and breathing cut off, both men choked for the want of air. Labounty felt his heart pound in every part of his body and his head was growing light. He knew his strength was all but gone. Bracewell's power was equally diminished - but there was no stopping, no quitting and no one would interfere. The final moment was here; it was as the old Chief had said, fate would be decided by their own hands.

Both men felt their legs weaken and simultaneously dropped to their knees, but neither lost their grip. Death was but seconds away. Labounty felt faint and the sounds of the crowd around him had begun to grow distant. How Bracewell felt he could not be sure. He too was weak but perhaps he would prove to be the stronger man. Labounty tried tightening his grip, but the strength was not there.

He had been wounded several times during the war but never had he been this close to death. Strangely, in his head memories began to flash, exploding at incredible speeds. They were vivid pictures of places he'd been, things he'd seen and people he'd known. It was an endless nonstop burst of things long forgotten. And while his fast-fading eyes continued to stare into the face of the man killing him, he somehow relived each and everyone. Then came a vision of Cub and Kay and Socorro; the three of them sitting about a campfire talking and laughing. For a second Labounty smiled, and unable to explain it, something took place inside him.

Abruptly the visions ended and like a shout from someone unseen, words of the old Chief burst inside his head; 'from the heart will come the true warrior's strength'. Bracewell was the darkness the old Chief had talked of, and although uneasy with the thought, Labounty realized he represented the light. In his heart he did not want to kill. And yes, Bracewell deserved to hang, but hang only after a fair trial.

Yet, regardless of what he felt or believed to be right this was an event of no choice, only one of them could leave the circle alive and ahead of Bracewell lay a continuing life of murder, rape and countless other atrocities to mankind.

Labounty closed his eyes, called upon the Maker for strength than reopened. Upon his face was an expression Bracewell could not recognize. The killer stared into his eyes and for the first time in a life of being the most feared, of always taking what he wanted and always winning, he knew this time he was going to lose.

Labounty tightened his grip and Bracewell felt pangs of fear. His eyes bulged excessively and he tried tightening his own clutch, but the strength was not there. They had been so equal in power and strength this entire fight for life, but now suddenly he seemed to be no match.

In desperation Bracewell let go of Labounty's throat and grabbed at his wrists to break his hold. But it was no use. He wanted to tell Labounty to stop, that he really did surrender this time, that he'd rather hang than die here and now, but he couldn't talk and the power in Labounty's hands felt unstoppable. In disbelief Bracewell felt blood begin running out of his mouth and heard the crushing of bone in his neck. His eyes fluttered and his face turned to fear, it was then that darkness of death came…it was over.

Labounty let the body fall into the dirt and with conscious effort rose to his feet. When he did the crowd roared and broke the circle running to his side. Just as they reached him his head spun and knees buckled. Toppling onto his side blackness came in the form of a welcomed, and long needed sleep.

It was three days before Labounty recovered enough to ride out with his friend. On the morning of their departure the old Chief presented him with a horse to ride, a gift. And while bidding him good-bye he spoke softly, "And so you see Labounty, it is as the ancestors of the Blackfeet have always believed, that in the end the good will win. I knew the battle would be a hard one. But unlike your enemy, you listened. And so, from within came the strength you needed. Know this, the power of this wisdom has given new birth to an even better warrior."

The old Chief turned then and grasped Socorro's shoulder. "May the spirit be with you on your journey of peace. Remember, my lodge is open to you. To you both." He glanced at Labounty, then back, "Now go, and each do that which waits for you to do."

Yuma was hot and the sun shone brightly as they rode together into town. Labounty had not looked so bad since the days of the war. Socorro rode beside him poised in the saddle, a proud and noteworthy man.

Slung across the back of a third pony was the body of Bracewell. His remains would be turned over to the Sheriff for proper disposal. They would inform him of the killer's recent crimes, especially those leading to the unjust killing of the farm couple and treatment of the innocent Hopi family because of it; and he would certainly be told of the wrongdoing going on with Kay.

Labounty rode with eyes alert, despite lingering swelling. Somewhere in the bustling little town a small boy and a beautiful woman were waiting. The air was hot, and dust stirred from the constant traffic of horses, buggies and loaded wagons. On both sides of the street citizens strolled along the narrow sidewalks as shopkeepers swept their storefronts.

Somewhere down the street a blacksmith's hammer rang out above the noisy rumbling of passing wagons. Several drivers took long looks at Labounty's face, and it made Socorro smile, "I think they are happy they are not you my friend."

At the Sheriff's Office they were given the address of the couple believed to be Cub's Aunt and Uncle. And much to their surprise they had discovered there had been a reward out for Bracewell.

After telegraphing for identification on Labounty, the sheriff presented him with a bank draft of five hundred dollars. Captured following a string of murders and bank robberies, Bracewell had been placed in the Yuma Territorial Prison where he escaped in less than a year. No one had known anything of his whereabouts until now.

While Labounty had already thought of a good use for the reward money, it was the idea that Bracewell was no longer able to kill and plunder that made him feel better about having taken the man's life.

Just as Cub had said, his relatives were a family of farmers with a small spread just north of town. Following a short stop at the bank both men mounted and rode out for the Stewart Farm.

The Sheriff had told them the family consisted of Rob and Mary Lynn Stewart and five children, two girls, twins, age fourteen, a sixteen year older sister, older brother twenty-two, and the youngest, a boy of ten.

As he and Socorro approached the farmhouse Labounty felt butterflies, but kept it to himself. Just what it was that made him nervous he couldn't put a finger on; perhaps it had something to do with all that had been happening over the past week. While he was the same man he'd always been, somehow things felt different. Not in a bad way, just a different way. On the last 100 yards to the house, he gave thought to the idea.

Some pack-mule vacation this has been, he thought. Over the years he had survived four years of Civil War and countless close calls during the Indian Campaigns. But in just a weeks' time, he had faced the murderous efforts of Mountain Men, taken on the responsibility of a small boy, and met a city woman out of Chicago hunted by a group of hired guns. Labounty let out a soft sigh, and last of all, faught and killed the leader of that group in a not so easy hand to hand fight in the middle of an Indian War Party, who ended up practically becoming family. Labounty gave another sigh, this one topped with a smile of his new learned wisdom, that sooner or later his luck could run out, and, he wasn't getting any younger.

He had to admit though, Cub had managed to somehow reach into his heart. And Kay, well, Kay, was extraordinary; a lady filled with warmth and sincerity, he closed his eyes for a second, and she possessed one beautiful smile. As for Socorro, he had rekindled the memory and importance of the need for priceless, close valued friends. Indeed, what a week!

Strolling into the farmyard chickens pecking at the ground scattered, squawking as they ran from the horse's feet. Clothes hung on a line drying, and suddenly the front door burst open. Labounty left his saddle and met Cub halfway. Sweeping the youngster into his arms swirling him around. Kay remained on the porch, standing beside an elderly gray-haired couple. Her face was aglow, and she was smiling brightly.

Putting Cub down and not taking his eyes off her, Labounty walked to the porch where she stood. Stopping just in front of her he matched her smile then reached up and lifted her down from the porch. They embraced for a long while. The older couple glanced at one another and smiled tenderly. Huddled in the doorway of the house five children also watched, they too were smiling.

Socorro had dismounted to greet Cub and now stood with his arm around the boy. Together they watched Labounty and Kay. Cub looked up at his Indian friend and asked grinning. "Think they'll start smoochen' Socorro?"

The Indian laughed out loud.

"I do not know my little friend. But I think today a great decision has been made. I think you will not have to stay here and be a farmer."

"Why?"

"Look my little fiend," Socorro said with a grin, "they are smooching."

Cub turned to look and smiled wide. Pulling the big hat from his head he threw it up into the air and shouted so loud, it scared the chickens.

"HOT DAMN!"

THE END

Labounty

A novel by

A. Alex Come'

Summary: Labounty

How exciting it is to allow our imaginations to run free, to dream, to pretend in our thoughts; to be whisked away to another time, another place by a good book or magic of the big screen. We've all visualized ourselves a King, a Queen, a brave Knight, a First Lady, an Indian, a Cowboy, a Soldier, a Roman…and so it goes on and on. Limited only by what we allow ourselves to envision.

When we think of the wild west, we picture cattle drives, gunfights in the streets, noisy saloons, the rattle of wagons, stagecoaches, cowboys and of course the war cry of the Indians.

We often forget, however, that the real characters of the west, those pioneers and native Americans who so bravely opened our country as we know it today, were people just like ourselves; they laughed, they cried, they felt hot or cold, were educated or non-educated, they loved, hated, felt the pangs of fear and experienced the glories of bravery.

Labounty is one of the many stories of just such people, settlers of the wild west. It is an adventure interweaving the two worlds in which we live today…truth and fiction.